NATIVE TRIBUTES

GERALD VIZENOR

NATIVE TRIBUTES

‹|› HISTORICAL NOVEL ‹|›

WESLEYAN UNIVERSITY PRESS

Middletown, Connecticut

WESLEYAN UNIVERSITY PRESS

Middletown CT 06459

www.wesleyan.edu/wespress

2018 © Gerald Vizenor

Manufactured in the United States of America

Designed and typeset in Fairfield LH by Kate Tarbell

Library of Congress Cataloging-in-Publication Data

NAMES: Vizenor, Gerald Robert, 1934– author.

TITLE: Native tributes: historical novel / Gerald Vizenor.

DESCRIPTION: Middletown, Connecticut:
Wesleyan University Press, 2018.

IDENTIFIERS: LCCN 2018008567 (print) |
LCCN 2018014228 (ebook) | ISBN 9780819578266 (ebook) |
ISBN 9780819578259 (pbk.)

SUBJECTS: LCSH: Indians of North America — Political
activity—Fiction. | Veterans—Political activity—United
States—Fiction. | GSAFD: Historical fiction

CLASSIFICATION: LCC PS3572.I9 (ebook) |
LCC PS3572.I9 N38 2018 (print) | DDC 813/.54—dc23

LC record available at https://lccn.loc.gov/2018008567

5 4 3 2 1

IN MEMORY OF NATIVE VETERANS

of the Bonus Army

Contents

1 › Dummy Trout 1

2 › Diva Mongrels 10

3 › Tombstone Bonus 20

4 › Double Prohibition 28

5 › Bagman Civics 33

6 › Anacostia Flats 40

7 › Enemy Way 47

8 › Cortege of Honor 56

9 › Look Homeward 63

10 › Liberty Trace 75

11 › Night of Tributes 92

12 › Ritzy Motion 97

Dummy Trout

Dummy Trout surprised me that spring afternoon at the Blue Ravens Exhibition. She raised two brazen hand puppets, the seductive Ice Woman on one hand, and the wily Niinag Trickster on the other, and with jerky gestures the rough and ready puppets roused the native stories of winter enticements and erotic teases.

The puppets distracted the spectators at the exhibition of abstract watercolors and sidetracked the portrayals of native veterans and blue ravens mounted at the Ogema Train Station on the White Earth Reservation. The station agent provided the platform for the exhibition, and winced at the mere sight of the hand puppets. He shunned the crude wooden creatures and praised the scenes of fractured soldiers and blue ravens, an original native style of totemic fauvism by Aloysius Hudon Beaulieu.

The puppets were a trace of trickster stories.

Dummy was clever and braved desire and mockery as a mute for more than thirty years with the ironic motion of hand puppets. Miraculously she survived a firestorm on her eighteenth birthday, walked in uneven circles for three days, mimed the moods of heartache, and never voiced another name, word, or song. She grieved, teased, and snickered forever in silence. Nookaa, her only lover, and hundreds of other natives were burned to white ashes and forgotten in the history of the Great Hinckley Fire of 1894.

Dummy stowed a fistful of ash in a Mason jar.

Snatch, Papa Pius, Makwa and two other lively and loyal mongrels lived with the mute native puppeteer in the Manidoo Mansion, a shack covered with tarpaper near the elbow of Spirit Lake on the White Earth Reservation.

The lakeside house and place name were overstated in mockery, and yet that shack with a slant roof and two small windows became a monument of native memories, of the endurance of a gutsy native voyageur who tutored soprano mongrels and revived the magic of native puppets. The mongrels were natural healers and devoted to the motion of hand puppets, caught the sleight of hand, the tease, crux and waves of gestures, and retrieved the murmurs, wishes and whimsy of the silent stories and mercy of memory.

Dummy Trout mimed, cued, teased, and signaled at ceremonies, parties, parades, and reservation events, and forever doted on that eternal native spirit in the bounce, jiggle, and conscious sway of the hand puppets.

Dummy was a silent storier of truth.

Snatch, a blotched blond spaniel and retriever, was the only migrant mongrel from outside the woodsy reservation, and the nickname described a moody manner at meals, as he snatched food and ran away to eat. Snatch and hundreds of other mongrels were abandoned with horses, pets, and even houses, barns, chapels of ease, and costly machinery during the Great Depression. The land was timeworn, farm families were evicted, even grease monkeys were suspended, and for thousands of veterans railroad boxcars became homes.

The mongrels avoided the vagrants and roamed in packs to survive, but most of the twitchy mongrels, once favored as escorts in the outback, slowly died of hunger, or were tracked down as puny prey by other animals. Snatch was enticed by the voice of a coloratura soprano, as stories of his rescue were told many times, and wandered with caution to the recorded sound of opera music at the Manidoo Mansion.

Papa Pius was nicknamed in honor of the succession of popes, an ironic gesture of pagan mongrels and spirited hand puppets. Makwa, the native word for bear, was a noisy mongrel terrier, forever teased with a hefty name. Miinan, the word for blueberry, named for the color of her heavy coat, and Queena, a rangy reservation basset hound and golden retriever mongrel, nicknamed in honor of the famous coloratura soprano at the Metropolitan Opera, were the two musical mongrels at Manidoo Mansion.

Dummy saluted opera sopranos with two handsome hand puppets, and marvelous truth stories were told about the great performances of mongrel singers. The Debwe truth stories were innate native scenes and related to creature voices and the elusive tease of creation and memory, and the stories continued in the adventures of earth divers and native tricksters. The original truth stories were about the mystery of lumines-cence, that shimmer and natural motion of blue light, and about natives who once danced with animals and chanted to the clouds. Later the vi-sionary stories were told about totemic unions, erotic winks, and the com-mon tricks of creation. Debwe stories revealed natural motion, the flight of a native dream song, the touch and fade of winter, and the steady flow of the great river, and landed in a hand puppet show of operatic mongrels.

The two rough and ready hand puppets, presents to my brother and me, became our curious new voices as veterans of the First World War. The two puppets, in the care of my brother, first told stories of our coax and cover as veterans in the Bonus Expeditionary Force that summer at Capitol Hill in Washington.

By Now Beaulieu rode Treaty, a native farm horse, from Bad Boy Lake to the Exhibition of Blue Ravens at the Ogema Train Station. Treaty, once the wagon horse at the Leecy Hotel, slowly clopped along the platform. She pitched her head near the abstract watercolor scenes. The mongrels moaned in the presence of a horse but were not shied. By Now had served as an army nurse and was ready to march with us and other bonus veter-ans at Capitol Hill. Walter Waters, the inspired leader of the overnight Bonus Army, and thousands of veterans from around the country were on their way to demand a bonus payment from the United States Congress.

The Ice Woman, or Mikwan Ekwe, was an elusive winter menace, a native enchanter of quietus. She lurked around the woodsy lakes on cold and clear nights, a wispy shadow, and with erotic whispers lured lonesome native hunters to rest in the pure snow, a serene death with the sound of lusty moans, but since the fur trade, the waves of deadly diseases, shamanic deceit, wars, extreme economic depressions, poverty, and hunger, and with the scarcity of totems and game the old icy stories were reimagined without winter and told in every season of the year. The urgent croak of ravens in the paper birch and that native dream song of "summer in the spring" became our new stories to outlive the treacherous tease of winter and poverty.

Miss Heady, our language teacher at the government school, taught us the word "quietus," and she used that word in precise conversations.

Quietus was the absence of nature, never the scenes of bear walks or kill-deer deception, but she never became a government teacher to wrangle with wild creatures, furred or feathered, or to treasure the noise of the seasons. Naturally, she had never been enticed by the stories of the Ice Woman. Aloysius, my brother, actually painted a great blue raven named Quietus, the blue shadows of bloody broken wings over the heaves and mounds of snow.

Heady confirmed in every sentence that she was a creature of blood-line clarity, the quietus of eastern culture and manners, and concealed two eastern cats, fussy shorthairs, at her federal apartment. Domestic cats had never earned the character of mongrels, and not many natives nurtured indoor cats on the reservation, only lonesome widows who had returned from cities to federal musters, covenants of service, and treachery in the ruins of the white pine and liberty.

Dummy teased my brother and me with silent beams, tics, and puck-ers, and the gestures of the two puppets were wild, bouncy, and generous. The Ice Woman cocked her head, raised a spiky wooden finger, trembled, and then moved closer and caressed my shoulder. My entire body shiv-ered with the pose of that icy touch.

The Niinag Trickster bumped my brother on the chest and cheek with his giant wooden penis. The touch of the icy puppet was an ominous scene, and the punch of a wooden penis was quirky and comical, but not an easy story to relate with friends. These were the presents of the short, stout, and shrewd mute maestro of native puppetry.

Dummy handed over the two weathered puppets with a noticeable hesitation, and the uncertainty may have been second thoughts or a se-cret sense of native custody. Rightly, that gift of puppets was a waver in a world of chance, but never a slight. Pussy Beaulieu, her great aunt, had carved the two puppet heads from fallen paper birch, and the crude clothes were fashioned with remnants of mission vestments and school uniforms. The Ice Woman wore a silvery smock with crocheted hearts on the sleeves, and the huge wooden brow of the puppet was painted white, nicked and stained with age. The Niinag Trickster wore leather chaps, a bisected breechclout, and a green fedora with a curved brim. Black fe-doras were the fashion of native men at the time. The trickster carried a medicine pouch and a wide black sash decorated with blue beaded flowers. Trickster characters were imagined scenes of sexual conversions in some truth stories, bold, cocky, chancy, and capricious, and at the same time the brazen puppet feigned vulnerability in hand gestures and jerky motions.

Dummy guided my hand under the silvery smock of the risky Ice Woman, and with the steady frown of a shaman she slowly aimed my fingers into the hollow head, sleeves, and blunt hands. The fingers were gnarled willow twigs. The puppet came alive in my hand and waved at the priest and station agent on the platform, and then pointed at each abstract painting in the Blue Ravens Exhibition mounted at the Ogema Train Station.

The Ice Woman was once an incredible creature of the winter nights, and at the train station that afternoon the puppet inspired memories of winter in the spring with the slightest hand motions, a hasty bow, jerky turns, a wave of the head, and teases with an erotic shimmy. No one escaped the mighty gestures and enticement of the Ice Woman.

Dummy backed away from my hand gestures.

The Ice Woman raised a wintery hand, waved a stick finger, and asked the mission priest if he had ever dreamed about a rest in the snow, an eternal slumber in the paradise of winter. My first voice as an icy puppet should have been more enticing, elusive, at least a lusty tease, but instead the words were taut, an uneasy parody of vaudeville. The priest excused the caricature and leaned closer to the puppet in my hand. "Yes, once or twice near the mission, enchanted by the whispers in winter trees, and the heavy waves of snow over the graves," he confessed, in that new game of puppets at the station. The Ice Woman pretended to be demure in my hand as the priest reached out to favor the wind checked birch head of the creature.

The Ice Woman turned away.

The Jesuit priest was an unusual missioner with a sense of chance, of humor, and he seemed to appreciate the native decoys of nature and nurture in spite of my clumsy puppet parody. He was short, wore a biretta and cassock, a more distinctive costume than the stern and steady Benedictine priests who ruled Saint Benedict's Mission on the White Earth Reservation. The Benedictines banished the puppets and strained to favor the abstract images of blue ravens, and a priest once urged my brother to more accurately represent the carrion crow as black, black, black, not blue. Most of the priests were truly wounded by credence, burdened by the culture of sacrifice and churchy colors, scared by the bold swagger and steady throaty croak of ravens at the mission cemetery. The priests were forever separated from creative scenes, the eternal natural motion of the seasons, and blue ravens in the sudden glance of morning sunlight.

Salo, the stout station agent, was a raven crony who shared his lunch with ravens and practiced the mighty croaks, but he was anxious around priests, and he was doubly shied by the strange gestures of puppets. He worried that puppets were shadows and souls of the dead, and ruled the world with jerky motions and satire. He knew my brother and me as war veterans, of course, and some twenty years earlier as the native boys who hawked the *Tomahawk* newspaper at the very same Ogema Train Station.

Salo turned away that afternoon to avoid the priest and our puppets, and pretended to examine the art more closely. He studied the shadows over the stadiums of war, fractured faces of soldiers and animals in bold colors, the double faces of the fur trade crusade with bright broken brows, cracks, creases, and distorted gestures of native soldiers as abstract blue ravens at the platform exhibition.

Aloysius, who could not escape the nickname Blue Raven, changed the style and form of his earlier ravens, the once great abstract blue wings with traces of rouge were revived with bold colors and broken portrayals, the natural motion of expressionism, the visionary sublime, or original totemic fauvism. My brother read newspaper stories and art magazines about modern art, abstract expressionism, the cubist teases, and together we visited museums and galleries in Paris at the end of the First World War.

Blue Raven was inspired by the dreamy traces and scenes of Henri Rousseau, the marvelous portraits, feisty faces, cerise lips, and the bold gawky features painted by Chaïm Soutine, the enchantment of colors and shapes by Henri Matisse, and, of course, the memorable, visionary, and naïve primitivism of Paul Gauguin.

Blue Raven was a spirited painter, and forever haunted by the crevice of nightmares, the broken scenes of memories, and dead totemic animals of the dreadful fur trade. He was tormented with the war scenes of humans and animals and created abstract blue ravens and fractured scenes of bold colors, an original style of totemic fauvism. The scenes were contorted motion, the maelstrom of natural motion with traces of animals, birds, and humans in the guise of ravens.

Marc Chagall painted double faces in motion.

Henri Rousseau created great forests of motion.

Blue Raven created the clout of natural motion and the truth stories of totemic fauvism. The French fur trade was an eternal cultural shame, and yet the memory of totemic animals continued as a source of stories and images in native art and literature.

The totemic images in my stories were more sublime than fauvism, and the animals were envisioned with the sway of poetic scenes, an ironic tease, the surreal words of description, and traces of visionary motion, that cosmic motion revealed in the expressionism of ancient rock and the cave art of our ancestors.

Salo praised the creative visions of my brother, "the fury of blue ravens, the bright colors and scraps of soldiers," great abstract wings and "unearthly crimson claws," and the station agent generously repeated scenes, to be fair in his favor, from my stories about the ruins of war and the later encounters with surreal and subversive art and literature in Paris.

Aloysius was directed to insert his fingers in the head, hands, and giant penis of the Niinag Trickster. He actually thrust his hand into the floppy puppet with a great gesture of confidence. He raised the wooden penis and shouted out comments about the sexual nature of totemic art and the lusty turn of seasons, nippy at the start and then a warm breeze with balmy seductions. Churchy art, the puppet shouted, was bloody, erotic, perverse, and the sacrifice of virgins. The most erotic and ironic native stories were about the giant penis of the trickster. The mission priests, nuns, missionaries, and native converts shunned the trickster and never ventured to repeat the lusty niinag stories.

The priapic trickster was overturned by the aroused heft of his huge penis in many versions of the lusty stories, and in other stories the trickster pecker was envied as a weather vane, ensnared with a shaman in a hollow tree trunk, captured by a hungry bear, the steady stump for a kingfisher or a paddle in a birch bark canoe, and a niinag disguised as a handsome lover in the natural, native course of jealousy.

Tricksters were always in motion, the natural motion of seasons and most stories, and the risky scenes were about incredible vitality, wily earth diver creations, magical and awkward conversions and sexual routs, mercy mockery, and hoaxers of jealousy. The ruckus created in trickster stories was never resolved with clerical or moral lessons, except in those chaste and heartless translations by early discoverers and righteous missionaries. The most erotic trickster penis stories were denatured by the romantic guardians of native cultures, and by the federal agents of decorous and devious assimilation policies.

Dummy was once captivated by words, entranced as a child by chant and chorus, and truly aroused by the voices of coloratura sopranos. She was inspired by the operatic sound of some words, the tones and sentiments, such as the last rose of summer, precious heart, the tender hand that rocks the cradle, old men and rivers, and the moody native dream songs, summer in the spring, beautiful as the roses, and the sky loves to hear my voice. Since the savagery of the firestorm that turned her love to white ash she mouthed the poetry and operatic arias only in silence, and was moved to tears by the voices of sopranos, but she never voiced a sound herself, not a single note or word, no rumors, rage, whimpers, whispers, or promises. Instead, she trained two tuneful mongrels to read the sly gestures of the opera puppets and to then sing, or rather bay and moan in various tones and unusual harmonies.

Dummy never regretted her silence, and she never carried a notebook to explain her presence. Pussy was concerned, however, and mounted a blackboard on the door inside the Manidoo Mansion. Only one message remained on the blackboard for more than thirty years. "The body is a great mystery, not the noisy words, not the blather of a congregation. Puppets tease the motion of the body, not the words, and tremble with the soul not the seasons. Listen in silence and you might hear stories in the motion of the puppets."

Dummy directed the diva mongrels with waves and jerky motions of the soprano puppets, and more vitally with the deft gestures of a raised eyebrow, a pucker, and the count of puffed checks. The spirited union of loyal mongrels and native hand puppets was an original tease of creation and tradition, an obvious truth story. Dummy was derided by the enemies of silence, and by those natives who envied her secretive manners. She was cursed for the mere presence of hand puppets, a deadly union, and mocked for the jerky motion of the puppets. The mute puppet master was a great visionary of silence and praised as a shaman of liberty, a brave mute with music and mongrel healers. Dummy was the hushed storier of puppet divas and the natural motion of the seasons.

<| 2 |>

DIVA MONGRELS

Dummy carried two puppets with perfectly carved birch faces in the wide sleeve pockets of her smock that afternoon at the Ogema Train Station. The names of the diva puppets, Geraldine Farrar and Alma Gluck, were world famous sopranos of the New York Metropolitan Opera. The great mouths of the sopranos were painted bright red, and each puppet wore a dark blue turban. The Farrar puppet was fashioned with embroidered crimson images of the cross and crown on the border of a stained altar cloth. Gluck wore a silk chiffon gown with a gold metallic floral weave that was tailored from a remnant of exotic cloth delivered some twenty years earlier by the old trader, Odysseus.

Odysseus traded fabrics, absinthe, and peyote.

Dummy raised Alma Gluck to her breasts and with hand motions and silent facial gestures directed Miinan, the great blue mongrel singer, to moan, groan, and bay a worthy version of "Old Black Joe," the popular parlor song written by Stephen Foster.

Salo, in spite of his resistance to puppets, returned to the circle to watch the silent hand gestures and hear the marvelous mongrel bel canto arias and recitals. Miinan raised her blue furry head, turned to the side, and wailed the detectable sounds of two words, "heart" and "gone," and the other words of the spiritual were so familiar to the audience that the blue mongrel actually seemed to chant the first four lines of the woeful song.

Gone are the days when my heart was young and gay,
Gone are my friends from the cotton fields away,
Gone from the earth to a better land I know,
I hear their gentle voices calling "Old Black Joe."

Salo, By Now Beaulieu, the priest, the federal agent, the medical doctor, my brother, and more than twenty natives and others at the Blue Ravens Exhibition that afternoon joined the mongrels and sang the chorus with reverence, *I'm coming, I'm coming, for my head is bending low: I hear those gentle voices calling "Old Black Joe."* The station singers were melancholy at the end of the song, and praised the passion of the blue mongrel and the puppet named Alma Gluck.

Dummy puckered her eyebrow, as usual, and then bowed twice with the gorgeous hand puppet. The golden flowers on the chiffon gown shimmered in the sunlight. Miinan wagged her blue bushy tail, raised one paw, and bayed. The Ice Woman was outshined by the spiritual song and turned away. The Niinag Trickster never missed a chance to posture, and saluted the soprano three times with his giant wooden penis.

Salo turned his back on the trickster.

Queena, the second diva mongrel, a basset hound and golden retriever mongrel, circled the station agent with heavy ears and a steady slaver, and then she waited with absolute composure for the hand puppet gestures to start the second concert that afternoon at the train station. Geraldine Farrar, always the prima donna in the tease and grace of an embroidered altar cloth, emerged from a wide pocket on cue with a slight whisper, and then the station audience heard a steady mongrel croon of the nostalgic song "Long, Long Ago" written almost a century earlier by Thomas Haynes Bayly.

> *Tell me the tales that to me were so dear*
> *Long, long ago, long, long ago*
> *Sing me the songs I delighted to hear*
> *Long, long ago, long, long ago.*

Queena waved her ears and puckered to moan the refrain "long, long," and then muted a melodic bark of the single word "ago" in the song. Her spirit and voice were gentle, sentimental, an operatic mood that was characteristic of some reservation mongrels. The tones were cozy, and with heavy whispers, a natural repose of the basset hounds. Queena was the great diva voice of the hand puppets, and once or twice a week she rehearsed the repertoire of puppet shows and songs on the shores of Spirit Lake.

Queena was a direct descendant of a celebrated mission hound at Saint Columba's Episcopal Church on the White Earth Reservation. The Episcopal vicar erected a cattle fence but could not contain with wire or any churchy favors the spirited basset hound, and the consequences a decade later were houndy mongrels, the natural union of untold golden retrievers, spaniels, terriers, pointers, beagles, bulldogs, and showy empire chow chows. That communion of particular brands, breeds, and native couriers created a truly marvelous natural selection of clever mongrels, and most majestic was the hand puppet singer. The godly missions were obviously more memorable and enlightened with the reservation match and breed of hounds and mongrels than with overnight conversions, salvation, and the stale bait of monotheism and bloodline assimilation of natives.

Dummy listened to recorded opera and popular music on a Silvertone hand crank record player that she ordered from Sears, Roebuck and Company. She was the only native on the reservation who recognized the names of great operas and distinctive sopranos. Every day she cranked the old phonograph to hear recorded music. Hand cranked because electricity was never connected to the Manidoo Mansion on the southwest shore of Spirit Lake. She heated the shack with wood fires, cooked on a cast iron stove, lighted a corner with kerosene, and listened to great sopranos in the steady glow of a single flat wick Aladdin Mantel Lamp.

Miinan and Queena, the diva mongrels, watched and remembered the hand gestures of the puppets and the puffy cheeks of the maestro, and practiced the sounds of the songs in front of the phonograph. Alma Gluck and Geraldine Farrar recorded hundreds of arias and popular songs on Victrola records by the Victor Talking Machine Company. The mongrels were captivated several times a week with the voices of great recorded operas, but the complexities of the music, coloratura sopranos, lyrical timbre, trills, tease and pitch, were beyond the range of the mongrels and the two divas of puppetry, such as the heady sopranos in *Madama Butterfly* by Giacomo Puccini, *Carmen* by Georges Bizet, *La Traviata* by Giuseppe Verdi, and, of course, *The Marriage of Figaro* by Wolfgang Amadeus Mozart.

Snatch nosed the soprano voices in the air but never whimpered or sang for meals. The divas were teased with treats, the same tasty deer joints and knuckles that the other mongrels were given after a special service. Native hunters once teased the retriever mongrels with treats, the very same practices of tricksters, truth storiers, and shamans.

The five mongrels heard the voices of Gluck, Farrar, Ninon Vallin, Mary Lewis, Lucrezia Bori, and Marion Talley, and at least once a night the unwound phonograph slowed the sound of the opera music and the mongrels mocked the weary and dreary recorded soprano voices with moans and poky bays.

Dummy was a shaman of the puppets.

Silvertone radios soon replaced the old phonographs, and the new machines cost about thirty dollars at the time from Sears, Roebuck and Company. Spirit Lake remained a hand crank culture without electrical power, and the radio broadcast of the long count fight of Jack Dempsey and Gene Tunney at Soldier Field in Chicago, and the coverage of Charles Lindbergh's flight from Long Island to France in the *Spirit of Saint Louis* were never heard by the silent puppeteer and five mongrels in the ruins of the white pine. The once recorded operas were soon broadcast on weekends across the country, but the magic of radios would never overcome the marvelously direct sound of music on the trusty hand crank phonographs.

The Metropolitan Opera broadcast the first radio opera, *Hänsel und Gretel* by Engelbert Humperdinck, on Christmas Day 1931. The opera could be heard on shortwave transmission, the Red and Blue Networks of the National Broadcasting Company, and on radio stations around the country. That first broadcast became a series of matinee operas on radio every Saturday.

Dummy was determined to hear the matinee opera on radio and persuaded John Leecy, with diva puppet hand gestures, to sponsor the first radio opera broadcast in the dining room of the Leecy Hotel. He owned one of the best radios, and the deserted hotel was the perfect place on the reservation to stage the first broadcast of the grand opera.

Messy Fairbanks, once the chef de cuisine at the hotel, was summoned from her home at Pine Point to prepare and serve dinner at the end of the radio opera. She had retired when the hotel closed but returned to prepare a sumptuous dinner, *lapin aux pruneaux en cocotte*, or rabbit stew with a marinade of fruity red wine, carrots, and onions, baked in casseroles with prunes, chicken broth, crushed cloves, and decorated with parsley.

The Jesuit missioner discreetly provided the red altar wine for the marinade, and the tasty, tender rabbit was served in carved wooden bowls. Dark beer, a secret home brew from a disguised brewery in the abandoned Motion Picture Theater, was served despite the obvious double prohibitions of the Eighteenth Amendment and the White Earth Reservation.

John Leecy and Messy had honored the native veterans of the First World War with the Banquet Français. The Leecy Hotel was fully booked at the end of the war, and the French cookery was known by hundreds of visitors who had arrived by train, many staying overnight for the delicious meals prepared by Messy. The stories of that great dinner at the end of the war, more than a decade ago, have become more spirited with recounting, and on that occasion we were two worried veterans, tormented with night terrors of combat, and at the same time we were teased and put right by the best healers on the reservation.

Odysseus, the trader, Augustus Hudon Beaulieu, publisher of the *Tomahawk*, Catherine Heady, the precise government schoolteacher, Damon Mendor, the only medical doctor at the White Earth Hospital, and the Benedictine mission priest, Aloysius Hermanutz, kindly diverted my brother, my cousin Lawrence, our close friend Patch Zhimaaganish, and me with praise and glory stories.

Misaabe and his tender mongrel healers Mona Lisa, Nosey, and Ghost Moth, transmuted the night terrors into the natural motion of dreams and visual memories, and restored the natural rift and fault of sounds. Memories of the Banquet Français, French wine, absinthe, and stories of war, literature, blue ravens, and the mighty mongrel healers, were resumed with the radio broadcast of *Hänsel und Gretel* that afternoon at the Leecy Hotel.

The Niinag Trickster was an erotic healer.

The matinee radio event was held in the hotel dining room with chairs placed in two curved rows. Some visitors had arrived from Pine Point, Callaway, and Naytahwaush, and the local guests gathered around the Silvertone radio console with the government teachers, the federal agent, the priest, and a vicar. John Leecy turned the gold dial, and tuned the green eye to the station.

Milton Cross introduced the story of the opera in a clear and evocative tone of voice. He praised the sopranos, and then actually escorted the radio audience, and our good company at the hotel, into the theater, describing the hush as the lights were dimmed, and the slow rise of the great gold curtains. We heard the soprano Queena Mario as Gretel and Editha Fleischer as Hänsel in the glorious matinee broadcast of the opera. Dorothea Flexer sang the fairy tale scenes of the Sandman, and the gorgeous soprano Pearl Besuner was the Dew Fairy.

The radio sound was clear but not as vital or perfectly pitched as the phonograph records of the opera sopranos. The transmission waves distorted the sounds, the sopranos wavered, but the static on records was steady. Miinan and Queena, the diva mongrels, were allowed to sit at the side of the dining room during the broadcast, and only once Queena raised her golden head and softly bayed in harmony with the well known opera scenes. The audience responded with easy laughter and then applauded the lovely mongrel rendition. The Metropolitan Opera was truly honored that night with the great cuisine at the Leecy Hotel.

The Niinag Trickster was reserved at the opera.

Dummy and the five mongrels were rescued from poverty and boredom by the hand puppets, and only the backward priests and adverse federal agents resisted the obvious spectacle and tricky parodies the puppets delivered to natives. She created puppets that had a greater sense of presence and character than the agents of the church and state. Only once the nuns invited the mongrels and puppets to stage a show at the mission school. The students were dazzled with the bouncy motion of the puppets and moved closer to imitate their gestures, and to mimic the chants, light moans, and sweet bays of the mongrels.

The mission students bounced with the puppets.

Aloysius Hudon Beaulieu, my brother, painted his first distinctive blue ravens on newsprint more than thirty years ago at the Ogema Train Station. That summer we waited for the passengers to arrive on two daily trains, and sold copies of the *Tomahawk*, the first independent weekly newspaper on the White Earth Reservation. I wrote my first stories that summer, the creative imitations of national and international news reports, and my brother created incredible scenes of enormous blue ravens perched on the trains, huge shadows of wings over the state bank, over the hospital, mission, and over the livery at the Leecy Hotel. Our uncle was the publisher of the newspaper, and we were paid for the sale of each copy.

The Ogema Station was always a place of quirky stories, imagination, adventure and irony. We pretended many times to board the trains to destinations outside the reservation, Winnipeg, Chicago, and once our uncle bought tickets for us to visit the Minneapolis Institute of Art. We were fourteen years old that summer, and named the tiny farm towns down to the enormous train terminal on the great Mississippi River. Eight years later we were mustered with our cousins and more than forty other natives to serve as combat infantry soldiers in the bloody First World War in France. The station had become a touchstone of original art by my brother, and my first written stories, and no one ever forgot that last poignant ceremony on the platform when native soldiers returned from the war with no certainty of citizenship. Nurse By Now returned from the Hindenburg Line with stories of wounded farm boys and her steady mount named Black Jack. The French truly honored us more than the government of the United States, and for that reason we enlisted in the Bonus Expeditionary Force and marched with thousands of other combat veterans at the Capitol in Washington.

Aloysius, my brother, became a distinguished native painter and his abstract blue ravens have been exhibited in Paris, Berlin, and Ogema. His original totemic fauvism, or abstract expressionism of watercolors and broken features of humans and ravens, started at the end of the war. The distortions, visual tone, and crash of colors were inspired mostly by the paintings of Marc Chagall and the elusive Chaïm Soutine. We had met these great artists in Paris.

My best stories started with our experience as combat soldiers, and later revealed the wonder, excitement, and uncertainty of expressionistic art and surreal literature in Paris after the bloody ruins of empire war, the low roads of enlightenment, and the deceits and swindles of civilization. My stories were published first in weekly issues of the *Tomahawk* and later as an edited collection in a newspaper magazine, *The Paris Fur Trade* by Basile Hudon Beaulieu. My brother and the other veterans on the reservation first nicknamed me the Furrier and later the Teaser. Furrier described the trade of words in my stories, and Teaser the play of scenes and characters.

Dummy and the two puppets, and many other natives, were at the station that spring to stand with veterans and to honor the memory of native casualties in the First World War. My brother painted bold abstract blue ravens in brutal war scenes for every native soldier and nurse who had served in the war. The totemic fauvist portrayals at the exhibition first appeared chaotic, fractured images of once familiar shapes and faces, frowns and smiles, and my brother refused, as usual, to explain the extreme forms and features compared to his earlier portrayals of blue ravens, those spectacular waves of blue ravens in various states of necessary rage, and with mighty claws and bold shadows over scenes of war and the reservation. *Totemic Fauvism: Faces of Blue Raven Veterans* was the first exhibition of art at the train station, and the original watercolors were only for sale to support native veterans on the reservation.

My brother had become a well known artist, but the market on the reservation for abstract expressionism and mainly his style of totemic fauvism was imaginary at best, and the actual market for expressionistic art of any kind was truly inconceivable for anyone but the very rich during the Great Depression. We were native veterans, an artist and a writer, with no chance of work or income on the reservation, and yet we were not authorized to leave without permission from a federal agent. The policy of consent was seldom enforced, a cruel irony of civilization and democracy. We created with paint and literary scenes an aesthetic liberty, but never pretended to be better than other natives or veterans. Yet we had original scenes and stories to deliver, truth stories of a totemic union of native memory and art. Nothing was more relevant at the time than a book, a painting, and the marvelous hand puppets.

Federal policies were withered promises.

The obvious burdens of the Great Depression were overcome with the spirited motion of the Ice Woman and Niinag Trickster, and several other puppets that my brother created later at the Bonus March in Washington.

The White Earth Reservation has always been at risk, because the separation of natives on federal exclaves was never intended to encourage enterprise, to nurture curiosity, creative art, music, or literature, or to

plainly advance the principles of justice and liberty. The nasty exclaves
were contrived to exploit natural resources at the crude expense of native totemic rights, but these predictable deceptions actually gave rise to
resistance and the steady subversion of federal policies.

The natives were dirt poor, several timber companies had cut down
most of the white pine, and the beaver and other totemic animals had
been decimated in the fur trade. The great comedown of the national
economy and the untold breadlines turned the cities into new reservations without the tease of treaties. Only the memories of bloody war
scenes changed our art, not the ironies of poverty. The older men on the
reservation were marginal trappers, and yet native families were steadfast
and supported the soldiers with the purchase of Liberty Bonds. Native
women who were too poor to buy bonds packed war bandages, and the
rate of native combat casualties was much higher than that of any other
order of soldiers in the First World War. More than the Germans, more
than the French, more than the British, but not more than the high casualties of the colonial soldiers from Asia and Africa, and never more
casualties than the African American soldiers who served in combat with
the mighty Harlem Hellfighters.

Native veterans, my mother, and thousands of other natives on reservations and in cities were flat broke at the end of the war, destitute ten
years later, and the apathetic federal government delayed the repayment
of the bond money and dickered with the bonus money promised to veterans of the war. President Herbert Hoover vetoed the whole bonus for
veterans and at the same time favored the rich, especially the millionaire
and financier Andrew Mellon, the United States secretary of the treasury.
The rich became even richer during the war, and workers who stayed
home were advanced with higher salaries at the same time that soldiers
faced the horrors of mustard gas and heavy artillery in combat. The very
same government that advertised national patriotism to recruit native soldiers, and then touted war bonds on reservations, carried out policies of
separatism. Most natives who served were not recognized as citizens of
the country. Later, the abuse of veterans and the veto of the bonus by
the president became the incentive to muster the Bonus Expeditionary
Force, a great bond of memories, truth stories, and soldiery unions of
culture, race, and liberty.

The union of veterans defied the politics of race.

Hermann Everhart, a retired bank president, one of the prosperous heirs of the war, proposed to purchase forty of the abstract blue ravens for an unnamed collector of native art through a gallery in Berlin, but the banker turned down the three abstract paintings that represented with names the native women from the reservation who had served in the First World War.

Blue Raven shunned the elegant banker that afternoon at the station and refused to accept the specific offer because it dishonored our cousins and the others. By Now served as a nurse and treated combat wounds on the Hindenburg Line. Ellanora Beaulieu enlisted as a nurse and was assigned to the American Army of Occupation in Germany. She served in a hospital, healed the enemy soldiers, and then she died of influenza in the same hospital. The painting in her name showed an enormous detached shadow of her broken face as a blue raven in flight over an ambulance and razed landscape, with heavy traces of rouge on the feathers. The blue shadow reached beyond the deckle edge of the paper, the features of a raven and human with no boundaries.

Everhart expressed his regret for the slight of native nurses, doubled the purchase price, and accepted the entire collection of original blue raven portrayals. He obviously was ready to pay more because he traveled with a wooden crate to transport the art. The abstract totemic paintings were packed and shipped by train to New York, then by a slow boat to Europe, and delivered to a gallery in Berlin, Germany.

‹| 3 |›

TOMBSTONE BONUS

The United States Congress passed the World War Adjustment Act on Monday, May 19, 1924. Five years and hundreds of promises after the armistice of the First World War, and hardly anyone noticed the war bonus legislation that most veterans turned down. The Bonus Act provided only limited loans, not a real bonus of cash, and the loans would be deducted with interest from final cash payment in some twenty years.

The Indian Citizenship Act was passed two weeks later, one more overdue bonus. Reservation natives were declared citizens of the United States of America. The act was ironic, of course, and with no trace of remorse. The provisions of citizenship would not "in any manner impair or otherwise affect the right of any Indian to tribal or other property." The white pine stumps, dams, and flooded wild rice beds were the ironic provisions of "other property."

The Bonus Act empowered tricky loans, and was rightly named the Tombstone Bonus because most natives would probably be dead by the time the government dealt with payments. Most veterans were on the road in search of a meal and a place to live and work years before the Great Depression, and on federal reservations most natives were the designated prisoners of poverty.

The United States Veterans Bureau was directed to deliver the Adjusted Service Certificates of the Bonus Act on the birthdate of each veteran, the pretense of a money gift. Government policies were seldom explained, and the reason certificates were delivered on the birthdays of veterans remained a great mystery.

White Earth Reservation veterans waited and waited to compare the birthday certificates. My certificate arrived two months after my birthday. Aloysius never received one, and later we learned the document had been delivered by mistake to Aloysius Hermanutz, the principal priest at Saint Benedict's Mission.

John Clement Beaulieu, my cousin, who had served with the combat engineers, raised a stink that the certificates were one more hoax of federal agents, and the government ruse became a game to create the most outrageous stories of the delayed secret birthday certificates.

Certificate names were erased in bright light.

Certificates arrived only on cloudy days.

Parchment certificates were used as ledgers.

Certificates were shunted in cattle cars.

The Ice Woman lured the delivery agents.

Hungry packs of mongrels ate the certificates.

Certificates were traded for white lightning.

Certificates were treaties held in trust.

Certificates were no better than land allotments.

My crafty bonus certificate was delivered on a cloudy afternoon, and with my name and the exact amount clearly printed on the parchment paper, but the provisions of the take back loan with interest were hard to read in the fine print. Truly, the great government hoaxers had prepared a late birthday Tombstone Bonus.

IT IS HEREBY CERTIFIED that pursuant to The World War Adjustment Act and in conformity with the laws of the United States, the amount named, FIVE HUNDRED AND SEVENTY FIVE Dollars, less any indebtedness including interest, lawfully incurred and due hereon, shall become due and payable on the first day of January 1945, to Basile Hudon Beaulieu, White Earth Reservation, Minnesota.

The certificate was payable after my fiftieth birthday, and the money would have lost value in that time, and most veterans were angry and rejected the deceit of a puny loan provided by the Tombstone Bonus.

The bonus was one more withered promise.

Dummy waved with the diva puppets in hand and the mongrels bayed on the platform that morning we departed from the Ogema Station for Washington. My brother had waited for me some twenty years ago to board the train for the first time to visit art museums in Minneapolis, the second departure from the station was our military muster to the war in France, the third was our search for work, and the last time we made tracks was our return to Paris the year Warren Harding was inaugurated president. He endorsed assimilation policies and undermined native water and mineral rights on the White Earth Reservation. We had returned to the reservation three years later when Harding died and the Congress passed the Indian Citizenship Act of 1924.

Salo issued special train tickets for Lawrence Star Boy Vizenor, Paul Plucky Fairbanks, Aloysius Blue Raven Hudon Beaulieu, and for Basile Hudon Beaulieu to travel from Ogema to Washington with a train change in Chicago. John Leecy paid for the train tickets, one more gesture of respect for our combat service in the war. Star Boy was an infantry veteran decorated for bravery, and Plucky was a native fancy dance soldier who earned his nickname for bold maneuvers behind enemy lines. He stole cigarettes, tea, biscuits, and potatoes from the Germans. Most of the plucky booty had been stolen earlier from the French and Americans. We were brothers, cousins, and outraged veterans on our way to serve in the Bonus Expeditionary Force, that crucial war between the bonus veterans and Herbert Hoover, the crude political engineer of the Great Depression and the president of the United States.

Blue Raven amused the children and their mothers on the train with the hand puppets. No, he never raised the pecker of the trickster, but instead he created the first hand puppet in our bonus patrol, suitably named Herbert Tombstone. The head of the puppet was made with a small condensed milk can, perfectly dented with bright eyes and a wide moustache scratched into the rusty metal. The droopy fingers were braided twine, and the presidential puppet was dressed in tatters, sleeves of rags, a chest of dirty velvet, and heavy canvas shoes. The hand puppet wore a red banner, "Tombstone Treaty Bonus."

The children on the train were truly enchanted by the presence of the ragged and chatty tin can, and the scenes of the hand puppet were more believable because most of the children were familiar with the Tin Man in *The Wonderful Wizard of Oz*, a novel written for children by L. Frank Baum. The train might have become the *Land of Oz* for a few moments between stations, and the children worried about the pet dog, Toto. We teased my brother because he was a very convincing tin head hand talker, and later he painted the bright Flag of Oz with the green star on the banner of the puppet named Herbert Tombstone.

The train swayed through the vast mausoleums of industry, gray, black, and shiny that afternoon in the rain, and abandoned with no shadows, no trace of urgency, no factory workers, and slowly clacked into Grand Central Station at Chicago. We had arrived on May 30, 1932, Decoration Day, in a station of stony stares, rumors, and the misery of the Great Depression. Yet there were ritzy women at hand with fur collars, and the moneyed men were dressed in tailored suits. Plucky named the dressy tourists the Puppets of the Pullman Cars. The men outside the station were downcast in gray fedoras and packed in rows on every shabby corner in the light rain, and downcast women hovered with their gaunt children at the entrance to the station, the untold sufferers of the dead economy.

Plucky waved at people around the station and worried when no one returned the friendly gesture. "Natives joke about misery, laugh over poverty, shout out at the bears, but even the smiles of this city have been stolen by Hoover and the monogrammed bankers of Wall Street." Not a single smile was visible, and we realized the futility of the hand puppets in the world of hungry strangers.

Chicago was a reservation of newcomers with no sense of chance or easy way to portray the contortions of empires, the brokers of democracy, and the native humor of poverty. The hand puppets were ready to treat and tease the children, but the elders were more prepared for vaudeville, popular songs, and crappy public poetry, than spirited puppet shows. The notable exception, we learned much later, was the grand Modicut Yiddish puppet theater created by Zuni Maud and Yosi Cutler in New York City.

Plucky was out of tune in the very city that was built with the white pine cut from the forests on the White Earth Reservation. He never attended a reservation government school, and his easy gestures were romantic, but mostly with a sense of irony.

Star Boy was distracted by the beggary.

An older man rested on a wooden case just outside the train station, chalky gray as the marble columns, and there were many stories about old native men with granite faces, but poverty was not the same in the city. The chalky man wore a threadbare suit, his black shoes were rough, oversized, the soles separated, and he smartly saluted my cousin Lawrence Vizenor. We were sidetracked by his generous manner, long gray hair, and toothy smile. Bright teeth with no caries revealed more about his stature than the suit and salute, more than shoes and posture. Somehow he seemed to know our cousin was a decorated veteran, but he did not know that my brother loathed the poetry the old man was about to read. At that moment the toothy man rolled his shoulders back and with a resonant voice recited selected stanzas of a timely poem, "Decoration Day," by one of the most famous poets in the nation, and truly despised on the White Earth Reservation, Henry Wadsworth Longfellow.

> Sleep, comrades, sleep and rest
> On this field of the Grounded Arms,
> Where foes no more molest,
> Nor sentry's shot alarms!
>
> . . . .
>
> Your silent tents of green
> We deck with fragrant flowers;
> Yours has the suffering been,
> The memory shall be ours.

A Wigwam Coffee tin was prominently placed on the wooden case with a neatly printed message, "Out of Work Teacher, Poems for Food." Plucky was captivated by the sound of his grand voice, the gestures of the old man, and the steady sentiments of the poem, but my brother was not ready to turn back our steady mockery of the poet and the mawkish images of the "tents of green," and the "foes that no more molest." The Civil War soldiers were dead and buried in parts with no names, and might rather decline the flowery bait of godly resurrections to escape the recitation of poems by Longfellow.

The teacher was prepared to recite selections from that lousy, disagreeable poem, "The Song of Hiawatha," created with Algic rumors and concoctions of native teases and the double takes of trickster stories, when my brother shouted out the first lines of the introduction to the long poem, the showy oratory of wigwams and traditions.

> Should you ask me, whence these stories?
> Whence these legends and traditions,
> With the odors of the forest
> With the dew and damp of meadows,
> With the curling smoke of wigwams . . .

Blue Raven chanted the next few lines of the poem with the old man, but the ironic courtesy was not mine. Their voices created a pleasant harmony outside the station, and several people paused to listen, and then dropped coins in the coffee can. I never forgot that our strict teachers at the government school required the students to memorize more than a dozen stanzas of "The Song of Hiawatha," truly unaware, of course, the poem was not related to natives, and Hiawatha was not Ojibway, Ojibwe, nor a native Anishinaabe. The poem was a wordy potion of a single god with no time or tense. I could not bear to recite the dopey sentiments and romantic deceptions of totemic animals in the fur trade, or the cover stories for the destruction of the white pine on the White Earth Reservation. I dropped two bits in the Wigwam Coffee can and turned away.

> *I should answer, I should tell you,*
> *"From the forests and prairies,*
> *From the great lakes and the northland,*
> *From the land of the Ojibways,*
> *From the land of the Dacotahs . . ."*

Hiawatha, my brother declared, would be a perfect name for a road puppet at the Bonus March. We walked around the train station, but the scenes of human misery were too much to bear with casual gestures, and we could not merely drop a coin in a hat or can.

The Capitol Limited departed late that afternoon, and the train roared slowly out of the station and through the remains of factories. Chicago was gray and desolate along the tracks. The landscape was in ruins outside the city, an industrial reservation with no glory statues or trace of flowers, no native tease of summer in the spring, and yet a young man was fishing in a heavy dead pond near a steel mill in Gary, Indiana.

The Capitol Limited, Baltimore and Ohio Railroad, from Chicago through Pittsburgh, arrived fifteen hours later at the Union Station in Washington. The train was truly elegant and expensive, and not the suitable move for the warriors of the Depression, certainly not for native veterans en route to the Bonus Expeditionary Force.

By Now was on the back roads with the wagon horse named Treaty, but most veterans traveled in boxcars and trucks, clunky cars, and others traveled with rock bottom fares, and some arrived on motorcycles or walked. We could hardly refuse the surprise gift of tickets for a sleeping car, and with sheets, curtains, and overnight services, provided by our friend John Leecy. He once hired my brother and me to work in the stable of the hotel, and then honored us as veterans with a banquet at the end of the war. He was right, we never would have paid the price of tickets on a luxury train.

The Capitol Limited clicked into the night.

The First World War came to mind with the sound of the train. The border of combat memories was never far away even a decade later, and especially that night as the steward, a veteran of the Harlem Hellfighters, seated us in the formal dining car. Henri, his train name, reminded me of the war because he wore a miniature Croix de Guerre on his white coat, a distinctive narrow ribbon of six wide green bars on a red background, the French military decoration for gallantry.

Henri was poised for service, precise, and courteous, the perfect steward of social status, and with a massive and toothy smile. He winked in silence when we noticed the medal and broached the war. No doubt he worried about four natives in the formal dining car, but we promised only the ironic war stories of cootie graves, *pinard, singe,* or monkey meat, not the bloody scenes, and we praised the courage and merit of the mighty Harlem Hellfighters in the Battle of the Argonne Forest. Henri told us later that he chose his train name to honor Sergeant Henry Johnson, who served with the Hellfighters and was decorated for bravery as a combat infantry soldier with the French Fourth Army. Henry was abandoned as a decorated veteran with many wounds, and he returned as a Red Cap at the train station in Albany, New York. He died alone ten years after the end of the war.

Lawrence asked Henri if he had ever met any other natives or enlisted infantry veterans on the classy Capitol Limited. The train rushed into the night of tributes, and his huge face reflected on the window between the pale lights of passing stations. "Gentlemen," he said with a slight bow, and then he moved closer, smiled, and continued, "you are the first Indians, but not the first savages to dine on this train."

My brother burst into laughter, and told the steward, "Now that we are actually wild citizens of this country, we plan to march with veterans and sentence the congressmen who voted against the quick bonus to live on reservations until the end of the Depression, and with the communists."

Henri turned away to welcome other passengers to the dining car. He directed two genteel older women to a nearby table. We were out of place by name and manner, of course, but our native stories of art, war, and literature were more creative that night than the social rank, gasps, and cultural blather we heard in the dining room and later in the lounge car.

The Capitol Limited was not a puppet train.

John Leecy, Salo, Messy Fairbanks, the chef de cuisine, and our relatives were celebrated in our stories on the road that night. Our stories were the continuation of the many versions of native road stories, and similar to the canoe stories of the fur trade. The versions and revisions of our truth stories were native traditions, not the mere recitation or pout of liturgy. Plucky mocked the rank and category stories of the burly men in the lounge car, the empire bluster stories, business associates in tailored suits, discovery of treasures, double dares of the stock market, and then he cast an ironic revision of the double prohibition stories on federal reservations.

We listened to lounge stories into the night and lightly teased each other over the disparities of the market values of government schools, and overstated the virtues and worth of the old hotel, the state bank, and dark depression theater on the reservation. Lawrence noted in a secretive voice, that he intended as a tease to be overheard, when he mentioned the understated value of the white pine stumpage, and then we returned to our bunks in the sleeping car as the train rushed through the dark heart of Ohio.

<| 4 |>

DOUBLE PROHIBITION

The Capitol Limited clattered over the bridge on the Potomac River at Harpers Ferry. The sunset raved in the oak and dogwood, turned the broken factories into hues of rosy bricks, revealed the fine white weave of tablecloths in the dining car, and two hours later the train arrived on time at Union Station near the United States Capitol.

The Capitol Limited never outran the misery.

Henri opened the carriage door and escorted the old women to the platform with a courtly manner, they were tourists and probably not aware that the city was occupied by thousands of veterans. We were the last to leave the train, and ready to start our road and totem stories in the Bonus Expeditionary Force. Henri saluted, leaned closer as we stepped out of the train, and then chanted a catchy line from a song in a musical, "Fifty million Frenchmen Can't Be Wrong."

Plucky, always canny and ready with a tease, returned the salute and crooned back a line from a musical he created overnight, "Four tricky warriors over there, and over here we are native veterans in the Bonus Army." The notions of the musical were delivered much earlier in the smoky lounge car when we overheard entitlement tales about the musical, *Fifty Million Frenchmen*, which first opened on Broadway a few weeks after the stock market crash. Two heavy barons of the lounge had free tickets to the witty production and recounted some of the scenes. The Paris of sex, art, wine, literature, music, and dance after the war was compared to the conservative monitors, churchy manners, prohibition, and tidy censors in the United States. Plucky was excited by the theater small talk, and with no knowledge of the musical, he cut in with a comparison of Frenchy lust and liberty to the tyranny of federal agents and the double prohibition of alcohol on reservations, and then chanted, "Ten Million Indians Can't Be Wrong."

The cadence of his voice quieted the dressy loungers. They probably had never considered natives in the public exchange of ideas, or cultural banter, certainly not about alcohol, and plainly reasoned that natives had a genetic weakness to firewater. No doubt they surmised the ten million vanished natives was a dummy boast. One rather stately man, who smoked thick cigars, and seemed to be connected in some way to the government, broke the silence with a simple inquiry, "Why a double prohibition?"

"Truly, sir, the prohibition was tripled because the agents outlawed alcohol on reservations long before the national prohibition." Plucky became the native courier of second thoughts, and with the sway of the train he held the attention of the other men for only a few minutes, probably because they were preoccupied with how a native could purchase a ticket on a luxury passenger train, and maybe they were distracted by our earlier tease talks in the lounge car about investments in timber stumps, banks, hotels, and theaters on the reservation. The white pine had been cut decades earlier, of course, and the bank and tiny theater had been closed for many years. Slowly the businessmen turned away, obviously not interested in the comparison, but the stately man asked one more question, "What then was the third prohibition?"

"Well, sir, you can drink, but not make or sell booze, but we were forbidden to drink hooch, make, or do anything with alcohol, unless, of course, you were a priest on the reservation." The other lounge men laughed about priests and altar wine.

Altar wine was a native communion.

Four veterans marched two abreast down the platform with the spirit of ravens at the very heart of the nation, and we were ready to overturn the delayed Tombstone Bonus. The steamy platform was a perfect scene for a silent movie as we emerged that night, the mysterious natives ready for political combat with the government. The Bonus Army was just one more adventure of native resistance to federal agents and government policies. Natives mocked the bloody quantum bunk, conspired to overturn the allotment of native communal land, declared the obvious with each breath, that natives were the first citizens of the continent and would outlive the pose and pack of the federal government.

Plucky marched directly into the central interior of the station and wheezed, wheezed, wheezed over the massive arches of marble, the empire center of worldly travelers, but we arrived that night ready for active bonus duty, not a tour of ancient architecture.

The station was crowded with hundreds of veterans, and almost every long bench was occupied with weary bodies, already slanted over for the night. We could easily recognize the veterans by their bags and packs, and many wore regimental insignias. Naturally we searched the rows of benches for natives or any veterans we might have served with in France.

We emerged from the station in the capitol night, with no idea of directions or a place to stay. The breeze moved the leaves and street trash, and with a strong scent of wood fires in the distance. We had no directions to name, and other veterans pointed to the south, so we started our walk toward Capitol Hill.

Plucky, the bold leader of our first bonus platoon, continued the merry march down Louisiana Avenue to Constitution and then to the National Mall. There were veterans camped in every direction from Capitol Hill to the Washington Monument, tents and shanties, fires, flags, dugouts, slogans and signs. We marched slowly through the thick smoke, canvas and cars, past state signs, and at last discovered five native campers under the banner of Oklahoma. The Cherokee veterans had arrived a week earlier by motorcar, a dusty 1929 Ford Model A, and staked a native claim on the grassy mall.

The Osage were nearby in two luxury cars.

Star Boy, our cousin, fought with Cherokee soldiers in the Meuse-Argonne Offensive, and now teased the veterans about the reverse of the Oklahoma Sooners, native land claims on the National Mall. We sat on the footboard of the car and on boxes and shined our stories for several hours that night. Plucky started to sing a chorus of the "March of the Hungry Man," and with original lines about veterans.

> *Give ear for the sound is growing*
> *From the desert and dungeon and den,*
> *The tramp of the marching millions,*

The march of the hungry men,
And natives from the reservation
Ready to march with the hungry veterans,
And overturn the bonus tombstones.

The Tombstone Bonus could have been the enemy way, a bogus bonus concocted by senators to deceive the veterans, but the capitol party hoax was revealed and became a great cause and union of veterans. That poetic tombstone would mark the political graves of the senators who had lost honor in the stories of veterans.

The First World War in France was never the same for natives, circles of race, breed, and colonial brands in combat, but the casualties increased with the hues and tones, and at the end of the war most native veterans returned to double exile on separatist reservations, and other veterans lost their jobs to younger men who were never mustered to serve in the Great War.

The Great Peace turned a blind eye to veterans.

The Cherokees were crowded under heavy tarpaulin, pitched and open at the sides, and the seats of the car were converted to beds for two native boys from New Mexico. Sergeant Counts, the father, was a veteran and native artist from Santa Fe, and his paintings were secured in the trunk of the car. He displayed his work every day at the Washington Monument, and in the previous few days he sold two portraits of Popé, the inspiration of the great Pueblo Revolt of 1680.

Counts praised our cousin Star Boy for his courage in combat and loaned him a heavy woven blanket for the night. The rest of us borrowed sections of double corrugated cardboard, not as cushions but as barriers to absorb some of the ground moisture that first night on the National Mall. Not the same as cold nights in the trenches, or the autumn forests of the war. Now we traveled with light clothes, no blankets, ammunition, thick coats, or rain cover.

Star Boy, Blue Raven, and I were awake most of the night, and so were hundreds of other veterans in the area. Counts had served in the same combat infantry regiment as our cousin. We listened to the stories nearby, and the sound of laughter in the distant encampments reminded us of the war, only the best memories of camaraderie and combat in France.

The footboard was more homey than a lounge.

Blue Raven never presented the hand puppets on the Capitol Limited. The stewards and porters were obsessed with service, and there were no children on the train. The upstart travelers were consumed with manners, not the right audience to imagine the slights and gestures of puppets in motion, but the children of veterans were ready to be doubly teased on the National Mall.

Herbert Tombstone pushed his tinny head above the car door and surprised the two boys in the back seat. The boys, ages six and eight, covered their mouths and giggled when the puppet shouted out that he was the only white man from New Mexico. "You know," moaned Tombstone, "the veterans kicked me like a can down the road to the White House." Blue Raven was perched at an angle on the footboard with the puppet over his head, and the open back window of the car became a perfect stage. "I lost my real head at a rodeo, and can you boys find me a place to stay?" His tin head knocked three times on the door frame. "Do you have a tiny bed for me in the back seat?"

The Counts boys were generous that night.

Thursday, June 2, 1932, was a cold and hazy night, and we counted the hours to dawn. The first glance of sunlight rescued our bodies from the overnight moisture, but the sun did not end our hunger. The camp was crowded and there were no spaces for the new veterans, only enough room for friends and family. Star Boy returned the blanket, the cardboard was dried out in the sun, and we were directed to a camp breakfast near Capitol Hill. Coffee, thick bread, and jam were barely enough to survive, but we were duty bound and ready to march or work for a meal at any kitchen on the road of the Bonus Expeditionary Force.

Counts named two camps nearby, a department store and a theater where bonus veterans were camped, and other veterans we met on the road mentioned Camp Marks on the Anacostia Flats. We set out to discover the veteran camps, choose our company, and connect with the skinny booted leader of the Bonus Expeditionary Force, Walter Waters from Portland, Oregon.

‹| 5 |›

BAGMAN CIVICS

Walter Waters was our guiding light and regarded as the mysterious premier of the Bonus Expeditionary Force. We were told he only attended large gatherings, and set aside more time for senators and sympathetic citizens than the veterans, but no one forgot that he secured most of the food for the Bonus Army. The veterans saluted the premier over the rutabaga soup and hard bread.

Waters worried most about the communists.

We were warned several times by veterans and police to resist the Communist Red Brigade, and especially John Pace, the Red Weasel, a leader of the commie workers and league of servicemen. He was a veteran poseur with a ready accent out of the Ozark Mountains. Blue Raven mocked the finger waves and empty words about commies. He drew a huge rosy head of a hand puppet and a red banner with the printed words, "Pozark Commie." Pozark, the creation of a hand puppet, was a combination of two words, poseur and Ozark.

Star Boy was in charge of our platoon that morning in search of overnight quarters, and aimed us in the direction south of Capitol Hill. We marched and played soldier down Pennsylvania Avenue to Eighth Street near the Navy Yard. The Bieber-Kaufman department store was in ruins, and fully occupied by hundreds of veterans. Bricks were stacked in the yard, barrels crowned with trash, and every room and crevice in the abandoned building was a strategic center of some veteran activity in the Bonus Army.

My brother searched trash bins and gutters on our patrols of overnight quarters in the city for tins, boxes, and scraps of cloth to make new hand puppets, and found everything he needed in the department store refuse, a red shirt sleeve, two shoe tongues, a bright tin of Union Leader Smok-

ing Tobacco with the image of a bald eagle, and Bears' Elephant Cigarettes, a matchbook holder, and various bits, buttons, shards, a necktie,
and string to create the red hand puppet named Pozark Commie.

The Bieber-Kaufman veterans, an integrated band of southern infantry
soldiers and Harlem Hellfighters, were invited by the owner to occupy
the ruins of the building. Most of the windows were out, entire walls had
collapsed, and yet the cracked cement and red brick dust was paradise
compared to the cold tamped grass at night on the National Mall.

The duty veterans at the store were concerned when they saw my
brother searching through the camp trash, and thought we were desperate and hungry. The veterans had no idea that we had traveled to the
city on a luxurious train, and had camped on cardboard for two days.
Grin Burns, a wiry veteran with a crooked smile, ordered us to rest, eat,
and smoke, and in that order. When he learned that we were natives
from the White Earth Reservation he shouted out to the other veterans,
"The Indians have arrived for the fight." Our presence was cheered, and
that became a natural bond, a residence, and regular meals for several
days. The dinner was an indescribable soup with rutabaga, cabbage, corn,
beans, carrots, and traces of stringy meat or some strange vegetable, and
the grain was earthy, but tasty, lasting, and truly a promise of survival in a
tin bowl. I was content with the trench soup, and the taste reminded me
of rough and ready meals in combat, prunes, potatoes, tomatoes, beans,
and weevils in the mushy oats.

Plucky traded cigarettes for four narrow sections of threadbare canvas
to cover the straw, enough to sleep on the concrete near the old load-
ing dock, and a few nights later we moved inside, to the second floor of
the department store. The toilets were slit trenches and covered dugouts
behind the building. Actually the second floor was not the best location
because the only access was a makeshift ladder, at night the only way to
the trenches and dugouts.

Star Boy was out at first light the next morning with several other veterans. They waited in silence, backs against a brick barrier, for the sun to
warm their bodies. Our cousin started the sun ritual when he was a boy,
and every clear morning since then he has faced the sun. He once told
me that enemy soldiers sought the same solace at first light, and then

turned back to continue the war. "I might have killed the same soldiers, but not at first light." Star Boy named the sunrise ritual the Enemy Way.

Pelham Glassford, the uniformed superintendent of police, arrived shortly after breakfast that morning on his blue Harley-Davidson motorcycle, part of a regular tour, we were told, of every veteran encampment in the city. He had provided tents, cots, and food, and truly worried about the hundreds of bonus marchers that arrived every day in the city. The veterans gathered around mostly to admire the motorcycle, but my brother saluted the former general and asked him about the other camps in the city. Glassford named Anacostia Flats, the National Mall, the Federal Triangle on Pennsylvania Avenue, and dozens of deserted buildings, and, for a few hours of sleep, he suggested the Gayety Theater on Ninth Street. He revved the motorcycle engine and continued his tour of the camps.

Plucky led our reservation platoon a few days later to the Federal Triangle, the first camp of veterans in the city, and where the veterans were mostly from southern states. Camp Glassford became the name of the encampment because the superintendent had directed the veterans who had arrived by foot and freight cars to that area of razed buildings and new construction. Hundreds of veterans were encamped there, and we met dozens of veterans who trained at Camp Wadsworth near Spartanburg, South Carolina, for combat infantry service in the First World War. Naturally, we told stories about the many pets, dogs, pigs, chickens, raccoons, and donkeys that some soldiers brought with them to the cantonment, the "Dere Mable" fictional letters in the weekly magazine named the *Gas Attack*, the simulated trench combat, and no rural boy would ever forget the peculiar gestures and military manners of the trench training officers from Britain and France.

My brother listened to the stories and at the same time created a crude new hand puppet with a white button nose, black eyes, and a curved smile scratched under the cameo image of a bald eagle on the tin of Union Leader Smoking Tobacco. "Pozark Commie" was printed on a red banner over a soiled canvas cape, and a shoe tongue headdress was attached to the top of the tobacco tin. The bottom of the tin was cut and bent open, and the cape was stuffed into the space so a finger could move the head of the puppet. My brother carried the hand puppets in a narrow case over his shoulder. Bonus veterans were never turned away, so we decided to stay for several nights in the ruins of the Federal Triangle.

William Hushka, the first veteran we met in the ruins, watched my brother create the puppet, and he applauded the first gestures of Pozark Commie. Hushka had emigrated from the Republic of Lithuania and served in the infantry in France. Puppets were everywhere when he was a boy. He told my brother about puppet shows in the parks of Kaunas.

Pozark Commie looked around, bowed to Hushka and the other veterans, and then the puppet turned around and watched my brother thrust his other hand into the tin head of Herbert Tombstone. At first the two puppets shunned each other, and then with a clank of tin heads, argued about war, revolution, money, labor, and peace.

Herbert Tombstone declared the Federal Triangle a new treaty reservation, a secure place to hunt and fish in the remains of the fur trade, and to chase rabbits, commies, and federal agents.

Pozark Commie shouted that Herbert turned his back on veterans but never resisted the touch of a rich man, not for any reason. The Tombstone tin head turned around and shouted that the commies were evil and destroyed democracy. "Look around you, this is our great rutabaga democracy," said Herbert. The veterans laughed, and then taunted the president, and others shouted back that they fought for democracy but got nothing back at the end, nothing but the deception of a Tombstone Bonus.

"I'm lookin' around and there are hungry veterans everywhere, cheated out of home and work by rich bankers and corrupt politicians, the bagmen of the democracy," shouted Pozark. Some veterans groused, and others might have agreed with the bit about rich bankers, but the veterans were patriotic and would never be coaxed by a tin head commie hand puppet to denounce democracy.

Pozark Commie jerked and turned away.

Herbert Tombstone waved to the veterans.

The Communist Party was not right about the war, or about democracy. Maybe some of the protests about the rich were right, but the commies were wrong about revolution and democracy. Most of the bonus veterans joined the Bonus Expeditionary Force to protest the delayed bonus, and never hesitated to shout out about the rotten policies of the government, but the veterans saluted the Constitution and democracy, and always carried at every march the Stars and Stripes.

Pozark waved the shoe tongue headdress and slowly looked over the few veterans that had gathered around the puppet show, but they were not yet ready to laugh, cry, or wrangle over the wacky statements of either tin head hand puppet.

> POZARK: Andrew Mellon owns the country.
> HERBERT: Joseph Stalin is a butcher of liberty.
> POZARK: Mellon owns stock in a distillery.
> HERBERT: Communism causes famine.
> POZARK: Hoover only rings bells for the rich.
> HERBERT: America is a country of opportunity.
> POZARK: Wall Street corrupted the world.
> HERBERT: France is always fussed with commies.
> POZARK: America could be great again.
> HERBERT: Not with a mob of commie veterans.
> POZARK: Better the mobs than a money Mellon.
> HERBERT: The Mellons built this country.
> POZARK: The monuments of poverty.

President Herbert Hoover and other elected officials and military officers used the very same word, "mob," to describe the veterans, a mob of agitators. Several veterans shouted back at the tin head puppet president, "The commies were chased out of our camps," and one veteran waved his arms and hollered in a southern drawl that when commies were caught they were tried, lashed, and banished forever from our bonus camps.

Pozark Commie stared down at the veterans.

Herbert Tombstone wagged his tin head.

The Communist Party was very active at the time in labor movements and protests, and veterans were warned that revolutionary commies might take over parades and demonstrations and turn the peaceful marches into violent protests against the government. "Our Bonus March is for the money, not a commie overthrow of democracy," said a veteran in the front row of the makeshift puppet theater in the ruins of the Federal Triangle.

pozark: Charles Curtis is a corrupt Indian scout.

herbert: Never for the commies.

pozark: Curtis scouts for bankers and breeders.

herbert: Soviet agents are your bankers.

pozark: Curtis is your bagman.

herbert: Stalin is your bogeyman.

Charles Curtis was a senator and then vice president of President Herbert Hoover, and was a native descendant of the Kaw and other native cultures in Kansas Territory. He never opposed the president, of course, but he faked support for the veterans and the demands for an immediate payment of the bonus money. Indian Charlie, an early nickname, did not inspire natives or the veterans.

"William Hushka is my good friend, he never was a commie," said Pozark, and turned to wave his arms under the canvas cape. The veterans laughed, and then shouted several last insults at the two tin hand puppets. Pozark Commie and Herbert Tombstone were returned to the puppet case.

Blue Raven was obviously excited about the playful responses of the veterans to the spontaneous puppet show. He chanced a few stories by the first hand puppet, the great present from Dummy Trout. The Niinag Trickster leaped out of the case and looked around for a few minutes at the veterans. Some veterans raised their fedoras because the trickster wore a green fedora and was dressed in leather chaps and a breechclout. The tin heads were retired for the day, and the veterans seemed more enthusiastic about the carved birch and painted head of the trickster hand puppet.

Trickster jerked his head to the side.

Plucky and my brother created a lusty trickster poem earlier on the train, and the hand puppet was ready to reveal the poem for the first time in public. Plucky pretended to be a ventriloquist and slowly recited the poem as my brother moved the head and body of the trickster puppet.

some god created this
heaven and earth
light and night
water and land

adam and eve
teases and totems
birds and animals
beavers and bears
cranes and cockatoos
snakes and snails
and a giant trickster dick
that keeps the whole thing going

The veterans heard the tricky lines of creation and watched the hand puppet gesture and move with the words, and at the end when the trickster raised a giant wooden dick several times, the veterans roared with laughter and slapped their thighs, and two veterans threw their fedoras at the trickster. Plucky chanted the trickster creation poem once more. The hand puppet jerked around with the words, and the veterans were ready for the trickster encore of the giant trickster dick.

Dummy Trout, the native shaman of silence and hand puppets, came to mind that afternoon. She created scenes of silent words in motion, a hand puppet pantomime, and with the barks and bays of mongrels. Dummy could move an audience with precise puppet motions, and create a sense of presence in the silence of poetry, but the trickster dick was a gesture of the sublime.

Dummy Trout inspired my brother to create hand puppets with the character of silence, and the gestures were visual and more memorable than poetry. My brother was an artist with the motion of hand puppets on the road, and a writer was necessary in the new world of native puppetry.

<| 6 |>

Anacostia Flats

By Now Beaulieu rode the old wagon horse named Treaty for more than a thousand miles over two months that late spring to march with the other veterans of the Bonus Expeditionary Force at Capitol Hill in Washington.

Most of the bonus veterans traveled in open boxcars, coal cars, livestock cars, others in rickety motorcars or farm trucks, and a few veterans rode motorcycles to the march. Some Oklahoma native veterans drove fancy cars, the oil discovery cars, and wore ceremonial feathers. By Now, no doubt, was the only veteran and nurse mounted on a horse along the dusty country roads to Capitol Hill.

Treaty was spirited and ready to tread, slow lope, and canter out of the stable and south along the river, and then east on the section borders of family farms. By Now and her steady mount were treated to supper and a stable almost every night on the back roads. Many farm boys had served as infantry soldiers in the war, some were wounded, and the families proudly supported the veterans and the Bonus Expeditionary Force.

Treaty pitched her head on parade.

The Anishinaabe were hunters and fur traders with canoes. We were not a horse culture, but that did not stop federal agents from sending treaty horses to natives on the White Earth Reservation. Fur traders teased the agents that they had cut holes in the bottom of canoes for paddle horse voyageurs. Mostly the horses were used to tow white pine logs and wagons, but not many plows. Our cousin easily learned how to ride and shoe a horse.

By Now toured the entire reservation on a Morgan, a chestnut wagon horse named Stomp, and with the doughty company of Torment and Whipple, two loyal mongrels. She was twelve years old at the time and trotted through rows of white pine stumps from Bad Boy Lake to White

Earth Lake, Naytahwaush, the headwaters of the Mississippi River at Lake Itasca, Bad Medicine Lake, and Pine Point, then returned by way of Callaway.

By Now was born late, more than a month late on the conception calendar, so late that her father boasted that she could speak several languages by the time she was delivered one warm spring morning. "That child should've been here by now," her father shouted over and over, and she was born a few hours later. By Now was her native nickname at delivery, of course, and later the catchy byname was entered as a given name on the federal birth certificate, By Now Rose Beaulieu. She has told variations of the same story, that there was no reason to start out in the world on the last few cold days of winter, so she held back her native arrival for a month to the first warm and friendly day in March.

By Now was born in a tiny house on Beaulieu Street in Ogema, and lived there most of her life, but she decided to name Bad Boy Lake, located a few miles away, as home when she was an army nurse because the soldiers were curious about unusual place names, and that was always an invitation to create unusual stories about the lake. She related the sudden turn of seasons, the spectacular natural scenes on the reservation, the mysterious healer Misaabe and his incredible recovery mongrels at Bad Boy Lake. Later, she declared that the old natural healer had inspired her to become a nurse. Misaabe was a small, easy, and elusive native who moved with the sound of whispers, and he encouraged my brother and me to create new stories to overcome the nightmares of war. The stories included the shadows of other creatures, the totemic dance of flies, the loyalty of ants, the steady wave of birds, and the inevitable teases of his healer breed of mongrels.

By Now was a veteran of the Army Nurse Corps and had treated hundreds of soldiers with combat wounds, and at the same time she had treated and shoed a few military packhorses in the First World War in France. Black Jack was the name of the horse she rode many times into combat near the Hindenburg Line, in violation of direct military orders, to treat scared soldiers with severe facial wounds from the heavy enemy artillery. Black Jack learned how to high step over the mounds of debris on the roads, the obstacles that blocked the ambulances.

Black Jack, named in honor of General John Pershing, was her favorite mount between the combat areas and the medical aid stations, and she rescued many other horses with combat fatigue. She trained the horses to carry out the wounded, and the soldiers reported that the steady sway of a horse was the calm after a storm, and much more curative than the noisy and bouncy ambulances overloaded with bloody bodies.

The soldiers teased her about the native equestrian style because she hunched so close to the withers and crest, and many soldiers were ready to mount and ride with her on any weary packhorse in the company. The farm boy soldiers were forever beholden to the nurse who rode a horse into combat with tourniquets, splints, compress bandages, and native medicine stories to treat their bloody wounds.

By Now should have been decorated for her courage, obviously, but the distant commanders avoided any official mention of the native nurse, the name of the horse, and the unauthorized combat duty. The French Army commanders, however, honored the unique medical services by a native nurse on horseback and awarded her the French Croix de Guerre.

Black Jack was a standard army horse.

Treaty was a wagon horse of liberty.

Treaty was a direct descendent of the original federal treaty horses, and was given to my cousin as a native tease. Treaty was once a wagon horse named Orchid, the last of the breed to serve overnight guests at the Leecy Hotel. Treaty was sidelined in the hotel stable, and with the arrival of motorcars and no wagon to tow or children to carry in circles, she was ready to escape the outdated wagon duty as a new native mount of favor on the country roads to native liberty.

By Now was the first veteran to leave the reservation for the Bonus March. She read about the move of veterans from around the country and could not wait to depart, but the tour by horse was much slower and safer than jumping boxcars. She departed shortly after the exhibition of blue raven art at the Ogema Train Station, and two months later we traveled by train to march with the Bonus Expeditionary Force.

By Now related later that Treaty had raised her head and cantered over the Potomac River on the Arlington Memorial Bridge, and then resumed a slower gait through the campsites on the National Mall toward Capitol Hill. She dismounted to talk with three veterans near a shanty named the Dug Out. We recognized the place, and the veterans told her about the schedules of the bonus marches, and warned her several times to watch out for the communist troublemakers in the camps.

By Now walked and Treaty clopped at her side down Constitution Avenue in search of water and a shady place to rest. Pelham Glassford, superintendent of police, drove by on his blue motorcycle, and then a few minutes later he circled back and parked on the sidewalk. He asked where she hailed from, and naturally she said Bad Boy Lake. My cousin was reminded that horses were not allowed on the National Mall or Capitol Hill. Glassford explained there were plenty of other places in the city to park a horse.

By Now was directed to the veterans at the Federal Triangle a few blocks back on Pennsylvania Avenue, or even better she could ride over the wooden drawbridge to the bonus camp at Anacostia Flats. Glassford told her that Anacostia was a real native place, with a river for Treaty.

The dopy guards at the entrance to Anacostia Flats waved Treaty and my cousin straight through the gate with no doubt or fear of commies. The guards were convinced that commies would not ride horses, and were only men, and they were probably right about the horses. Most of the commie veterans were big city boys, and the only horses they saw were in movies or the mounts of policemen.

Treaty was reined to a bench outside The Hut, a huge green canvas sanctuary that was started by the Salvation Army. The Sallies, dressed in neat uniforms, had set up a library, provided tables to write letters and play games, and gave away shoes, clothes, playing cards, and tobacco to veterans.

By Now seldom read literary stories or novels. She would rather create her own stories, and yet she was an obsessive reader of newspapers. She read twice every single page of the *Tomahawk*, the very newspaper our relatives had edited and published on the reservation, and later on she read every article in the newspapers cast aside by travelers at the Ogema Train Station and Leecy Hotel. The news stories were a rush of gossip, she said, and with "no tease or humor." By Now was a true native storier because she envisioned the scenes of the newspaper accounts and then related a more ironic and memorable story.

Charles Curtis, for instance, was on her mind about four years ago when he was elected as the vice president. Herbert Hoover was the moneyman and food huckster, and hardly noticed natives or the distant ancestor of the vice president, White Plume of the Kaw. By Now read the stories in newspapers about the candidates and the election and created new ironic stories. Curtis was born in a territory not a state. By Now teased that his mother was a prairie caption of the Kaw, Osage, Potawatomi, and French, and his father was a migrant merger of the Scottish and Welsh, a territorial fur trade rivalry on the run in the blood, bone, and beard of Charles Curtis. He raced horses, rode bareback, and learned how to whisper native promises in the ears of the horses, and with enough oat mush, rich grass, and prairie liberty to win money at races. He whispered and the horses would canter or dance. The political whisperer could have been a circus barker.

Curtis was named a senator, and his strategic whispers of legislation amounted to nothing for natives but an empty chair of manners. He shouted out an act in the Senate that overturned treaties and natives lost their rights to horses, land, timber, and minerals. White pine reservations became timber stump estates.

I became a writer partly by reading and imitating the style of some stories in the *Tomahawk*, and encouraged By Now to write about the war and her service as a nurse, but she was a creative storier not a solitary scribe, and she was more vital on the back of a horse than cornered in a library with echoes of editorial chatter, grammar, and literary points of view.

Swat Beaulieu, her father, blurted out "by now" as a constant native tease, rather a mastery of the moment with blunt "should haves" and closed with a signature "by now." "You should've worn a dress by now," and "You should've settled down by now," and "You should've found a husband by now," and "You should've had children by now," and most recently, "You should've written books by now."

By Now wore trousers, even as a child, and never owned a dress, except as an army nurse, but even then she wore trousers under the long dress uniform. She was nourished more by natural motion than by men, and would rather ride a good horse than run with a man, but she almost married once, and we forever teased her about the soldier who tracked her down on the reservation.

Le Caporal Pierre Dumont, an infantry soldier, followed her home from the Hindenburg Line in France. Nurse By Now had hoisted the wounded soldier onto a horse, and that lift, a memorable touch, became a fantastic romance for the lonely French soldier, and several months after the war he arrived healed and lusty that spring in search of our cousin on the White Earth Reservation. We pointed him in the direction of Bad Boy Lake. Pierre was enchanted by the romance stories he had read about natives and especially the mawkish novel *René* by François-René de Chateaubriand. Louisiana and Minnesota were distinctive states, of course, with only the Mississippi River as a connection, but that was close enough for the corporal to satisfy his wild romance with a native woman of a fur trade culture.

By Now would never marry, but she never hesitated to carry out the memory and lusty motions of the ancient fur trade with the French. The steady sound of his gratitude, and the rush of her laughter, created enough gossip to last a decade, but not the actual union. Pierre returned to his family fish market at Les Halles in Paris six months later, only hours after the second wicked snowstorm. He wailed that his bones were frozen, and he was terrified by the native stories about the Ice Woman.

Pierre wrote three postcards, nothing more.

By Now walked Treaty down to the river, and from there she could see in the distance the dome of the Capitol Building. Treaty waded in the shallow water, and pitched her head from side to side. Later, she rode back to the camp, and searched for a familiar face, or a practical place to stay for the night.

By Now talked to a boy with a pudgy dog about the word "Bonus" printed on the sides of a pet vest. She leaned over and asked the boy if Bonus was the actual name of his dog. The boy was shy and silent, but he was very excited and reached out to touch Treaty. She asked once more, and the boy said, "No, my dog is named Geronimo." He always wanted to sit on the back of a horse. By Now asked his father for permission and then raised the boy on the back of Treaty. He held the reins, and By Now led Treaty slowly around The Hut. Pudgy Geronimo barked at the horse, but Treaty was steady and only moved her ears. Other boys gathered and wanted to ride, and two girls who were not shy about horses, and they were eager to ride. Treaty was gentle, more content in the camp of bonus veterans and their children than she had ever been in the stable at the Leecy Hotel.

By Now was relieved to see my brother and me at the library in The Hut. Star Boy and Plucky were nearby talking with a group of veterans. By Now moved slowly from behind and surprised me, and then Aloysius. I was reading a copy of *Three Soldiers* by John Dos Passos. We turned and shouted out her name loud enough for everyone to hear, and then we danced in the aisle of The Hut.

Treaty neighed close by.

The White Earth veterans moved to the high benches and waited in line for a meal that early afternoon. Plucky asked By Now about the long march from Bad Boy Lake, and she told several stories about the back-yard veterans on country farms. They wanted to march with the Bonus Army but could not leave because there were crops to harvest and too much seasonal work on the farm.

Johnnie Eyespot, the nickname of one farm veteran, was ready to ride, walk, or bounce with the Bonus Army at Capitol Hill. He lost his right arm and eye in combat near Château-Thierry. He was badly scarred from shrapnel, she related, and yet he was eager to march with the bonus veterans, but could not find a horse to borrow. His labor was slight with one arm and one eye, and he wore a mask over the right side of his face with a huge blue eye painted on the crude beige canvas. By Now said she raised some money from several families for him to travel by train, and promised to look after the disabled veteran at the Bonus March in Washington. She had asked several veterans that morning about Johnnie Eyespot, but only one person remembered the farm boy with the owl eye and a canvas mask. Eyespot had been seen at an encampment near the bridge with other wounded veterans near Capitol Hill.

<| 7 |>

ENEMY WAY

Star Boy captured the enemy way at first light, and for thousands of other veterans the rapture of a sunrise would ease the night memories of war. The crack of flares, artillery thunder, and the sound of machine guns came back at night with the turn of an eye. The deadly tone of voices and the bloody dance of enemy soldiers continued in the haze of nightmares, and with the torment of faraway curses, duties of death and shame.

The Bonus Army beat the count of war.

My cousin was decorated for bravery in combat, and when he returned to the reservation he goaded the federal agent to create a common way to honor the veterans who weathered the nightly scenes and scares of war.

The warm waves of first light became his solace of the enemy way. That silent motion of creation every morning carried away the nightly torments of combat, the fury of memory, the bloody rage and traces of enemy soldiers on his hands and face, and with every cue of military tributes.

Star Boy envisioned the enemy way.

William Hushka and other veterans were calmed that morning with a clear sunrise, a natural union of the bonus warriors. Some veterans were never out at dawn and yet were ready to envision the same favor and union at sunset. Hushka led us to a camp supper, and stories of the enemy way continued over slippery dumpling soup, chunks of potato, and a hard biscuit. We drank the gray broth and with our fingers scooped the rest.

Hushka rushed the supper stories to show us a perfect pile of bricks with a magical view of the sunset over the Federal Triangle and Pennsylvania Avenue. The red bricks were stacked in the shape of benches, and naturally we asked who built the park lounge. Shanks, an out of work bricklayer, created the contoured benches for a marvelous sunset. The bricks were set and fitted precisely for the comfort of veterans. He was an infantry sergeant who lost his left leg at Château-Thierry.

Shanks deserved the sunset bench of honor.

Plucky sat at the side, ready for the dusk.

The camp stories continued into the blue night.

Hushka was from the Republic of Lithuania, moved from Saint Louis to Chicago, and then served with the first combat units in France, and to boot he was one of the first veterans to arrive in the city. We became close friends that night, and he told generous stories about the secretive Walter Waters and the politics of the Bonus Expeditionary Force.

"Lithuania, how do you get there?" asked Plucky.

"Baltic Sea," said Hushka.

"Savage kingdoms," shouted Shanks. "Demons with royal banners, terrible place, my family, we were dirt poor and migrated to a farm of liberty in North Dakota to escape the demons of the German Empire."

Hushka recounted the fear and hunger of outsiders, refugees in their own homeland before the Great War. "The Russian Empire, Prussia, and Habsburg Austria divided our country, and drove out thousands of Lithuanians."

Plucky mentioned the Spanish, British, French, and Russians as rival stories of the cruelty of discovery and colonial occupation of native communities, but only the migrant versions of empire ruled that night.

"Americans are scared of communists," said Shanks. "Europeans have always worried more about the border countries, the empires and fascists, than the heavy headed turnout of the Communist Party."

"France is menaced by fascists and communists," said Hushka. "Joseph Stalin and his cutthroats could wreck the country, every country, and who would care?"

"Léon Blum," said Shanks.

"Germany would care," said Star Boy.

"Japan, maybe," said Plucky.

The sunset barely calmed the newcomers.

The stories about the cruelty and comedy of military commanders continued into the tender night, and nearby the money packer president was served dinner on precious porcelain with state sycophants at his side, and downed expensive and prohibited brandy in crystal glasses at the White House.

Star Boy and other decorated veterans were directed by the Bonus Army to wear their medals and decorations for bravery, the Distinguished Service Cross, and French Croix de Guerre. Walter Waters, high booted in a bow tie, was featured as commander in chief of the Bonus Expeditionary Force. The former sergeant from Oregon ordered decorated veterans to muster at the front of every march in the city.

Star Boy never boasted about his service or decorated civilian clothes with war medals, and he refused to march at the front of the column for any reason. He balked at the order because native veterans were not there to prove a rank or course of bravery, or display ribbons of courage at the front of parades. The heavy memories and tributes of war were personal, not patriotic cavalcades.

Premier Waters posed as a politician.

I was the leader of our foursome native platoon the next morning. We walked down Pennsylvania Avenue and Eleventh Street to the Navy Yard, and over the river on a wooden drawbridge to Anacostia Flats. The name of the river and place was derived from Nacotchtank, the natives who once lived and traded in the area, and scarcely survived the diseases of discovery, colonial removal, the catch and catechism of missionaries, and outright murder. Centuries later the traces of natives continued as mysterious veterans in the capitol city of a constitutional democracy. The Nacotchtank natives were embodied in our memory and the history of the Bonus Army at Anacostia Flats.

Blue Raven and Star Boy abruptly turned around in anger at the entrance to the encampment because veteran guards demanded discharge documents to prove we were veterans. Communists were not allowed at the camp, and the dumb guards believed the absence of documents would reveal covert agents of the Soviet Union.

Plucky demanded that the guards prove that they were actually veterans. "I think you might have been touched by the commies on your way to the latrine," shouted Plucky. The guards were flustered and backed away, probably worried that we were either police or military inspectors.

Blue Raven was on the drawbridge when we shouted out that the problem had been resolved. "Alas, the gate chief ruled we were not real commies," said Plucky. "He said we didn't dress like the renegades." The police had scared veterans into believing that some gang of commies was about to take over the camps. There was no way to tease the guards, no easy native mockery or play to reveal the stupid notions of a revolution at a dusty camp of veterans. Plucky raised his fedora to the guards, and so we did the same, a native tease of haute couture and hat dissent.

"Commies wear red underwear," declared Plucky.

"Caps are subversive," said Star Boy.

"Communists never wear fedoras, a dead give away," said Blue Raven. "You know, commies wear flat hats, hide in trees, very nervous out in the open, and they set out to sabotage every wooden drawbridge in the country with safety matches." The guards waved to enter the camp.

"Indians, many around these parts?" asked Plucky.

"Only some from Oklahoma," said a guard.

"Indians own this place, you know, so you better get your ass ready to return our land," said Plucky. "You have no right to guard our land, and you owe us back rent, roughly three thousand months for stupid squatting without a native license."

"Glassford told us to guard the camp," said a guard.

"We want our back rent bonus," shouted Blue Raven.

"Yes, we want our native land bonus," we shouted over and over at the nervous guards. "Give us our native bonus, this is our homeland."

Anacostia Flats was a vast realm of transient veterans encamped in canvas tents, wooden shanties, slanted covers, and motorcars. Several thousand veterans mingled on the dusty roads, and more shelters were erected from scraps of lumber and canvas since we crossed the drawbridge. Plucky saluted the veterans and children as we wandered around the nests and hovels of the Bonus Expeditionary Force.

Circus tents, tiny tents, pitched boards, arbors, and curved boughs, or city wickiups, were crowded together at the camp. The Hut, a huge green canvas cover near the entrance, was started by the Salvation Army. The Sallies hovered around the library, and they were eager to give away cigarettes to veterans.

Plucky had small wide feet and was lucky to find a pair of comfortable shoes at The Hut. My brother found a light blue medicine bottle, the size of a puppet head, and scraps of tan and black cloth in a ragbag of giveaways. I looked at books in the library, mostly fiction, but we were only visitors at the camp.

Nearby a skinny entrepreneur sold hats, pans, shirts, tires, and much more, and there were other unusual scenes at every turn on the dusty tracks. "Alfred Steen, Bonus Soldier," was printed at the bottom of a "burial case." The veteran in a white shirt and tie was stretched out on a raised platform, and with this notice, "The most of us will be dead by 1945." The sign was an obvious reference to the passage of the Tombstone Bonus.

One barber cut hair on a dusty pathway, and names of the states were painted on posters, poles, and car doors. The Stars and Stripes waved at every dusty bend and warren of shanties in the camp. The hundreds of prominent flags were enough to scare the commies out of the country. "Maryland Vets," a large poster was set on top of the highest pole, and the camp was settled mostly by states. "Ogden Utah" was painted on the side of a car.

By Now had asked the same shy boy about the name of his pudgy dog with "Bonus" painted on a vest. We asked too, "Is that the name of your dog?"

"No, sir, my dog ain't no bonus."

"So, what's his name?"

"Geronimo," the boy whispered. He was worried about the name, surrounded by four natives, and turned toward his father. Plucky leaned over and cuddled Geronimo. The dog wheezed, and we moved to the next state circle of veterans, heard the freight train tales, country march stories, hunger jokes, dugout humor, the uncut names of generous citizens on the bonus road, and then returned to the happy checkers players on the high benches near the library.

The Hut was covered and more spacious, and a good place to rest before we returned for supper at the Federal Triangle. I searched once more the titles of used books, old novels, travel stories, classical histories, and picture books of circus freaks. I found an early edition of *The Odyssey*, and a copy of *Three Soldiers* by John Dos Passos. The First World War novel was published ten years earlier, a year before we left the reservation a second time and returned to Paris.

Dos Passos graduated from Harvard College and then served as a driver in the Ambulance Corps, along with many other young writers who avoided the military. I knew that much from newspaper stories, and he started to write about the war when he read *Le Feu,* a war novel by Henri Barbusse, the fierce veteran who first turned to lofty pacifism and then marched with the French Communist Party. I leaned against the book table and read at a glance a few scenes and some character chatter in the *Three Soldiers,* and was not taken away, but my criticism as a combat veteran was probably unfair because the war had ended more than a decade earlier. The novel was mostly dialogue, soldierly jargon, and with class clumsy accents. The slight notice of war noise and devastated landscapes would easily convince most veterans that the author was not a trench soldier, but an educated spectator or ambulance driver.

A Sally moved around the circus tent with absolute ease, and her casual manner turned the canvas cover into a home, parlor, and a library. She helped veterans write letters, and smiled when she noticed me standing nearby with a copy of *Three Soldiers.* "John Dos Passos was here today," she said, "writing something about the camps and working on a new book about big money." Dos Passos had looked over the same stack of books, she told me, and even his own novel.

Plucky saw Dos Passos near a Model A Ford talking to several veterans from Pennsylvania. We gathered around and listened to the conversation with Anthony Oliver and two other veterans. Anthony, a bricklayer, drove from Belle Vernon at the end of the school year with his seven year old sons, Nick and Joe. The boys were boxers and staged fights at the camp. Anthony mentioned that Pelham Glassford, the superintendent of police, and seven or more officers, played baseball with the veterans, and the regular games were one of the high points at Anacostia Flats.

Blue Raven opened his shoulder case to show Nick and Joe the three hand puppets, but he only steadied the two tin heads, Herbert Tombstone and Pozark Commie. The boys were amused when the puppets butted heads, and my brother encouraged the boys to actually say a few words for the hand puppets, only a word or two. "Butt your own head," said Pozark Commie. "Don't smoke," Nick said for Herbert Tombstone.

My brother raised a black cape and small blue medicine bottle and created Wizard Oil, a new hand puppet with jerky head motions. He spit in the dust, and with a muddy finger touched a mouth, horns, two eyes, and a curved smile on the blue face. The new puppet had just the right camp cures for cramps, headache, neuralgia, and toothaches, and to heal a lame back. The boys watched closely and backed away when my brother warned in a muted voice, "Wizard medicine no good for camp boys," and the blue head bowed and turned to the side. The boys were not shy but unsure about a native veteran who created crude hand puppets with rags, bottles, and tins.

Château-Thierry was mentioned, a catchword of the deadly war, in a conversation about the ambulance service and wounded soldiers stacked on the side of muddy roads. Dos Passos seemed at ease with the veterans, and he turned every combat notice around to lambaste the politicians and generals who carried out the war.

I asked Dos Passos about his novel *Three Soldiers*, and would he create the same scenes today, or does time change the perception of the author and the characters, more grave, more absurd, more humorous, and more philosophical? Anthony and the other veterans moved closer to hear the response of the author.

Dos Passos said his novels were chronicles of the time, not just fiction or history, but stories with a critical bent, and he used the word "bent" more than once. *Three Soldiers* may not be a good novel ten years later, he said, and pointed toward the library, but the story was one more record of war. He seemed detached, not quite there, as if his words were directed to some other conversation, or maybe an article for a magazine. He paused for a moment, and then said he had never forgotten the experiences, the smell of war that lingers in memory, the smell of poison gas and artillery explosions.

I continued with my questions because more veterans had gathered in the circle to listen. "You experienced the war as an ambulance driver, would your novel be more direct if you had experienced combat as an ordinary private, an infantry soldier?"

Dos Passos explained once more that his novels were chronicles, and some other novels about the war were preachments, authors must show passion and rage, but too much anger and emotion was a preachment, not a novel. He insisted, "My novels are not preachments."

Dos Passos seemed evasive, and the veterans were obviously thinking about personal combat experiences as soldiers, and the natural creative right of preachment about the dread and stay of nightmares of the war.

"Veterans forever search for the solace of the enemy way," said Star Boy. Slowly the discussion became more personal about the war, and distant from *Three Soldiers* and Dos Passos. The veterans responded more urgently and directly to the question about actual combat and the escape distance of an ambulance driver.

"I was a nurse and carried wounded soldiers out of combat on the backs of horses," said By Now. "Ambulances were noisy, unstable, and worthless when the roads were bombed by the Germans."

Dos Passos nodded in agreement.

"Ambulance drivers were never ordered to rush over a muddy pitch at dawn in the face of enemy machine guns," said Star Boy. "Soldiers were sacrificed by the orders of distant generals, and the ambulance drivers were never threatened with treason for a strategic turnaround to avoid casualties and an enemy camp. The war might have been a better chronicle as a constant preachment of combat soldiers."

Blue Raven said, "General Pershing ordered soldiers not to write about their combat experiences in journals, or even letters, because the generals worried that the humor and preachment of ordinary soldiers would counter the entitled military chronicles of the war."

Preachment was the word of the day.

Dos Passos was silent and then cut into the stories to say that he would sign a copy of *Three Soldiers* at The Hut. He was ready to leave the conversation about war and his novel. Sally was happy that we both returned to the library, and she carried out the usual service, no favor or special recognition of an author over a veteran. Dos Passos signed his novel in a practical way, not with the flourish of a vain author, and regretted that he could not dedicate the book to honor our conversation at Anacostia Flats.

"Send the library another copy," shouted Plucky.

"Dos Passos, would you do that?" asked Sally.

Naturally, the author could not resist the charge and promised to replace the library copy. He dedicated the novel to me, "Basile Beaulieu, Combat Stories at Anacostia Flats, June 10, 1932."

"By Now was a combat nurse," shouted Plucky, "not an ambulance driver, so you should include her name in the dedication." Dos Passos agreed and wrote her name on the title page.

I expressed my appreciation, of course, but his novel was not my choice of literature. I had memorized, however, a few sentences from *Three Soldiers,* and recited the lines at the right moment to surprise the author with one of his own scenes. "The company sang lustily as it splashed through the mud down a gray road between high fences covered with great tangles of barbed wire, above which peeked the ends of warehouses and the chimneys of factories."

Dos Passos seemed hesitant at times that afternoon, but never at a loss for words. Yet, to hear a slight wave of his own novel, a strategic delivery by a native veteran, truly took him by surprise. He was poised and grateful, and wondered how many other authors had been waylaid with selected sentences of their own work.

I had recited a passage only one other time, and that was from *Ulysses* by James Joyce at the first celebration of the novel with Sylvia Beach at Shakespeare and Company in Paris. Joyce was surrounded with too many artists and literary admirers, a bookstore overcome with the arrogance of clever creatures of art and literature. I moved closer to Joyce, leaned near his ear and whispered two lines of his new novel, "Pain, that was not yet the pain of love, fretted his heart." Joyce did not respond to my gesture of respect, but there was no reason not to continue, "Paris rawly waking, crude sunlight on her lemon streets." Joyce turned away slowly with a distant gaze.

Dos Passos turned and slowly walked down the dusty trail to the drawbridge. His shadow was narrow, and he might have saluted natives and veterans for their emotive memories and decent preachments about the war, because the chronicles of learned ambulance drivers were dead on the shelves of libraries.

By Now might never have read *Three Soldiers*, but the dedication to her by the author was a chance to boast, and she carried the book back to the White Earth Reservation.

<| 8 |>

CORTEGE OF HONOR

Star Boy recovered a sense of solace in the easy luster of the city that early morning. The great columns of elm trees were brighter in the rain. The federal buildings were mostly stone gray, but there were slight traces of blue and rouge in the windows, on the side of a bus, faces in the crowd, bright umbrellas, and the rain lasted the entire day.

Blue Raven was our rainy day platoon leader.

The Gayety Burlesque Theater was truly a vision of paradise, and the façade, stage, and grand balconies were reminders of the time we worked more than a decade ago at the Orpheum Theatre in Minneapolis. The classical statues over the grand entrance arch were shiny in the rain, and inside the heavy scent of velvet, cosmetics, and cigar smoke were cues of our theater memories.

My brother paused at the entrance to the theater, just under the back balcony, and we were overawed with the huge stage and three circles of balconies. The Gayety was a grand palace, and we decided then and there we wanted to work and live in the theater. Plucky turned around in circles and counted the statues in the arches over the balconies. The ornate curves, masks, and heavy decorations of ivory, gold, and empire red might have sidetracked a new performer.

By Now had never visited a burlesque theater.

Star Boy was ready to watch every show from the high balcony. Then, as we slowly walked down the aisle to the proscenium stage, we heard moans, groans, grunts, and muted snores in the back balcony. My brother heard more than grunts and snorts on the stage, he heard faint sounds and whispers in the wings. He was perceptive to the stay of theatrical voices in the circle, and the traces of passion and humor on stage.

Some players thought the theater was haunted.

Twelve years earlier we were hired as stagehands at the Orpheum Theatre in Minneapolis. We carried huge trunks for actors, moved stage property, constructed sets, and even raised the curtain for vaudeville situation
comedies and musical productions. The union was weak at the theater
and we were fired because we dared to return to the reservation for a fu-
neral. The manager would not be troubled with any personal diversions. A
few months later we returned to the streets and stories of Paris.

France was a theater of the fur trade.

Jimmy Lake, the owner and manager of the Gayety Burlesque Theater,
heard our voices as we walked toward the stage. We were seated on the
aisle when he walked on stage, stared as us for a few minutes, and then
pointed directly at Plucky, By Now, Aloysius, Lawrence, Treaty, then me,
and ordered the six of us to stand next to him on stage. We followed
orders and marched out of the wings and into the bright lights. Treaty
balked at the stairs near the side of the stage.

"Listen, do you hear snores?" asked Jimmy Lake.

"Yes, but more than snores," said Blue Raven.

"What, the ancient plumbing?"

"No, muted voices in the wings."

"What voices?" asked Jimmy.

"Mollie Williams in *The Unknown Law*."

"Yes, she was a racy player, right here on this very same stage maybe
ten years ago," said Jimmy. "How would you know about that playlet, were
you in the audience?"

"Orpheum Theatre in Minneapolis," said Blue Raven.

"Prejudice, war, movies, unions changed our world forever," I said to
suggest that we knew something about entertainment. "So, we left the
country, and my brother became a famous painter in Paris."

"Who rides the horse?" asked Jimmy.

"Me, only me," said By Now.

"Well, we could use a horse scene on stage."

Jimmy was distracted by the sound of veterans in the balcony, and
turned away. My experiences as a writer and soldier were too much to
consider as an introduction, but surely he was not surprised by actors and
overplays. We were on stage with a master impresario, and there was no
reason to be shy.

"You should see the puppets," said Plucky.

"Puppets, so what can puppets do?"

"Hand puppets, but not now," said Blue Raven.

"Why not, this is a theater," said Jimmy.

Aloysius was annoyed that he was being coaxed to display the puppets, and not at the best time, but he could not resist the chance to show a theater owner the puppets. He moved out of the bright stage lights into the shadows and raised on his right hand the Niinag Trickster. The green fedora on the carved head jerked to one side, then the other, and then the puppet slowly turned toward Jimmy Lake.

"Carnation Jimmy, the famous gold dust racy raconteur of burlesque and dancing girls," the trickster said in a muted voice. Niinag waved his arms in circles and moved closer to the impresario, close enough to almost touch his nose with the curved rim of the fedora. Eye to eye the trickster cocked his head and said, "Hire these five native veterans and a horse to work in your theater, or, or, puppets remember every slight."

"Aloysius made a puppet of President Hoover, a tin head named Herbert Tombstone," said Plucky. "He might turn you into a tin head puppet, but not if we get to stay at the theater."

Jimmy was amused, "What can you do?"

Niinag Trickster stared and said, "Aloysius, my hand brother, worked at the Orpheum Theatre in Minneapolis. Basile the teaser, my other brother, talked about the union and we were fired without notice or pay."

"The stage is out, solid union, what else?"

"Watch for dogs and boozers," said the trickster.

"Not sure, bootleggers might have a union."

"Stand outside with hand puppets?"

"Right, no puppet union yet," said Jimmy.

"I am the native union steward of veteran puppets, and these boys are honest workers, and turn on the lights with the best stories," said Niinag Trickster. "Treaty would bow and carry old ladies to their seats." He jerked, shivered, and moved into the bright stage lights. The trickster directly faced the impresario and raised the enormous wooden penis several times. The shadow of the dick was cast much larger in the stage lights.

Jimmy Lake doubled over with laughter, and when he recovered said we were hired to work until Congress voted on the bonus for veterans. Names were recorded, and then we asked about our duties.

"Full time, night and day, two veterans always on duty, make sure the place is secure," said Jimmy. "But the most important work is to watch over the platoon of veterans that sleep in the balcony."

The snores were real, not a stage play. Jimmy worried about veterans that arrived in the city with no place to sleep, so he turned over theater seats in the back balcony of the huge theater. One platoon would sleep during the day, and the second platoon at night. The arrangements violated the city sanitation laws, and city inspectors would surely evict the balcony veterans from the theater. Our duties were to be sure that no public official found a platoon of veterans asleep in the balcony. We would watch for city snoopers, and protect the sleepy veterans. Jimmy avoided contracts and paid us with meals, and we could sleep in a storage room at the back of the stage with the voices of actors.

"Wait," said By Now. "Daily oats for Treaty."

"Done, so get to work," said Jimmy.

‹   ›

Congressman Wright Patman, Texas Democrat and veteran, cosponsored legislation a few weeks later to provide a cash bonus to the veterans, and after many political tricks and diversions the bill was finally scheduled for a vote in the House of Representatives.

The theater veterans were out early to join the march, and not a snore could be heard from the balcony. Not one veteran remained in the theater, and our duty that morning was to march with the Bonus Expeditionary Force.

Star Boy was our platoon leader on that clear morning as we marched with thousands of other high point veterans down Pennsylvania Avenue to Capitol Hill. By Now saluted and Treaty pranced sideways at the head of the march with the decorated veterans. Everyone gathered on the steps, shouted, whistled, and waved hundreds of Stars and Stripes, state and city signs, and placard declarations, "Pay the Bonus Now And We'll Go Home," and "1917 Nothing Was To Good, 1932 Nothing Is Right," and "I'm Helping Daddy Get the Bonus."

I was overcome with the spirit of the march and waves of voices, songs, and hollers on the marble steps. My body was packed together with others, voices merged in stories and songs, and without notice or fear my sense of personal presence was no longer necessary. I was only conscious of the passion and motion of the veterans. I no longer had a sense of native distinction, and the other veterans close to me from Maine, Georgia, Mississippi, Louisiana, California, Utah, Oklahoma, Texas, and North Dakota, black, white, and disabled merged with the common motion of soldiers in the Bonus Expeditionary Force. That sense of union is a chance experience, once or twice in a lifetime, and endures only in stories.

Star Boy led our platoon through the sway of veterans into the Capitol Building and the public gallery of the House of Representatives. Commander Waters ordered veterans not to enter the gallery, but we were poised and sober, and decided not to attract attention by sitting close together. The veterans were there, of course, to witness the speeches for and against the actual bonus legislation, and especially to hear the great friend of veterans, Congressman Edward Eslick, Democrat from Tennessee.

James Frear, a congressman from Wisconsin, rose to the podium and dressed down the legislators, declaring that those who earned thirty dollars a day "should not denounce these wet, ragged, bedraggled men soaked for days in the rain, who only ask for a dollar a day." Frear was sixty years old and had served before the turn of the century in the United States Army.

Edward Eslick was the next representative to address the legislators. There was a clear view of the speakers from the balcony, but the veterans leaned closer out of respect to hear the great congressman. He gestured to his wife in the front row of the gallery, and started with an easy censure, "Uncle Sam, the richest government in the world, gave sixty dollars. Mister Chairman, I want to divert you from the sordid. We hear nothing but dollars here. I want to go from the sordid side," and then suddenly he turned silent, gasped, doubled over with pain, and collapsed on the floor. Congressman Eslick, the honorable advocate of the bonus money for veterans, died of a heart attack in the House of Representatives.

Plucky moaned, and waved his hands.

Blue Raven was the last to leave the gallery. He waited until everyone departed to the exits and then placed three hand puppets, Herbert Tombstone, Pozark Commie, and Wizard Oil on separate seats in the gallery. The puppets were seated in the front row with a view of the legislators. He fastened a note to each of the puppets, "Edward Eslick was a great warrior."

Star Boy and other veterans were devastated by the death of the veteran and congressman. The next day our cousin wore his Distinguished Service Cross, a reversal of an earlier decision, and marched in the cortège to honor the memory of Edward Eslick. Near Union Station more than five thousand veterans waited for the procession to pass, and the balcony veterans never returned to snore or grunt at the Gayety Burlesque Theater.

Wednesday, June 15, 1932, the cash bonus legislation was passed in the House of Representatives. The mighty roars, whoops, and hurrays reached across the city, over the drawbridge, and echoed through the marble hallways of the Capitol. Over the next two days more than six thousand veterans gathered around Capital Hill to demonstrate their support of the bonus and to wait for the delayed decision of the United States Senate. The veterans waited on the marble steps, and on the grassy mounds, and sang a new overnight version of the chorus to "Over There." The Capitol Hill revision of the George Cohan lyrics that night changed the "Yanks are coming" to the "Yanks are starving."

Over there, over there,
Send the word, send the word over there,
That the Yanks are starving, the Yanks are starving,
The drums rum-tumming everywhere.

Friday, June 17, 1932, the drawbridge over the river was raised and more than thirteen thousand veterans were held captive at Anacostia Flats. Superintendent Pelham Glassford learned about the bridge detention, and ordered the police to open the drawbridge. He declared the obvious, that veterans were not criminals and had a right to stay or leave the camp. The veterans marched directly that night to Capitol Hill.

Walter Waters, premier of the Bonus Expeditionary Force, was the first veteran to be informed about the late night vote. Waters, dressed in his signature bow tie and high boots, announced that the legislation had been voted down, defeated, and tabled by a vote of the Senate, but he shouted it was only a "temporary setback."

Saturday, June 18, 1932, we were depressed by the death of Congressman Eslick and angry about the defeat of the bonus legislation in the Senate. Most of the senators were rich cowards, men of money on the run, and they escaped through the back door to avoid the veterans on Capitol Hill.

Plucky marched our platoon in silence from the marble steps to Union Station. We cashed in our luxury return train tickets and bought cheaper seats on the first train to depart for New York City.

By Now declared that she would never leave the city without Treaty, and she would never ride alone along the railroad tracks and through the ruins of factories to be with her cousins. Yes, her reasons were absolutely the truth, and who would dare torture a gentle horse through the debris of dead factories. By Now was in love and would stay forever with William Hushka at the Federal Triangle, and in time he might decide to ride back with her to the White Earth Reservation.

<| 9 |>

Look Homeward

Aloysius outlined blue ravens at the march of the Bonus Army, and on the train that afternoon he turned the pages of the ledger book and told stories about the scenes. Blue ravens were sentinels on the drawbridge over the Anacostia River. Four ravens cast enormous shadows and feathery traces over the encampment on the National Mall, and hundreds of abstract blue ravens, the silhouettes curved and intertwined, were perched on the White House.

John Dos Passos carried a mishmash of blue ravens in an ambulance, beaks and wing feathers stretched out of the windows, and his name was painted on the hood. Blue ravens carried a streamer with the words "liberty trace" over the Federal Triangle. Plucky slowly turned the pages and laughed at the scene of the grotesque pear faced president, and blue ravens perched on the balcony over the veterans at the Gayety Burlesque Theater.

The *Columbian* eased out of Union Station in the early afternoon, swayed past rows of empty warehouses, and stopped at Baltimore and Philadelphia, and arrived four hours later in Jersey City, New Jersey. There were no porters in white coats, no tease or salutes on the gray platform, only the mingle and flow of passengers to the buses bound for Grand Central Station in New York City.

Aloysius used his finger to outline great raven wings on the dirty windows of the bus and then closed his eyes to avoid the fear of enclosure, and imagined the scent of a cedar grove as we entered the Holland Tunnel under the Hudson River and emerged on Canal Street. The bus slowly lurched along Park Avenue and parked at the terminal on Forty-Second Street. We marched with the other passengers to the enormous main concourse of Grand Central Station.

New York City was a heavy shadow.

The Roman gods, Mercury, Minerva, and Hercules, posed in mythic fashion over the outside clock and great windows of the terminal, and the scenes of dressy travelers, men in summer suits and women in slinky silhouettes, were mostly the descendants of chancy commerce. We were distracted by the poses of fancy people, the four faces of the inside clocks, the echo of announcements, and the whispers and chase of trains, and the incredible constellations painted on the curved ceiling were spectacular.

The great cavern was decorated with curved windows and ornate sculpture. The tone of echoes was distinctive, a signature of poise and plenty, the grace of time, and surely the soughs and promises of certain estates. The scarce sound of laughter came from a lounge of decadence. There were no traces of hungry children, or even the slight shuffles and murmurs of poverty. The economic depression, the stock and big money swaps, started downtown, and the casualties were always convened at a distance, two, three, five blocks, and hundreds or thousands of miles away. The ordinary cost of train travel was a luxury of time unimagined on the dusty plains of Kansas and Oklahoma, or in the ruins of white pine on the White Earth Reservation.

Dummy Trout would create a fancy hand puppet for the concourse event, a money maid dressed in high heels with fishy eyes and a fur trade collar, and with a tease of mercy and jerky moves she would direct the diva mongrels to bay the song, "Brother, Can You Spare a Dime?" The tease of a puppet maid came to mind the entire time we were in the city.

Four native veterans of the war and the Bonus March were marooned in a cavern of wealth and travel covenants, and yet we were at ease in the splendor of the moment, and the natural slant of light that early evening. The scent of concocted perfume was a chancy cue that we had landed in a strange dream song, and the clouds waited to hear our voices in New York City.

Grand Central Station was encircled with skyscrapers, the most recent erection higher than the others, and lighted at the pricey point to warn pilots, and maybe a just marker for the migration of geese. The art deco Chrysler Building was a block away on Lexington Avenue. The heavy marble monument, decorated with gargoyle hood ornaments, was a prominent tease of civilization and poverty, a precious stone statue built with the excess of money from the sale of costly cars. My brother touched the curves and colors at the entrance, and he was tempted to cut a native totem, sandhill cranes, or the figure of a trickster, in the polished marble.

Plucky was our platoon leader that night in search of cheap food and a place to stay. We marched to nearby Bryant Park and the New York Public Library. There were hundreds of downcast citizens, and surely many veterans, in a breadline that circled the park and continued along the elevated train tracks. We had money to eat, and would not wait in line for a meal that others deserved more. There were no overnight campers, so we continued north on Fifth Avenue to Central Park. Seventeen tiny rickety shacks were erected in what we learned later was named Depression Street in Hoover Valley. The area, once the park reservoir, had been drained and was muddy. We met only three residents at the encampment, and they were worried about the police. Naturally, one of the shacks displayed a large Stars and Stripes. Nearby there was a small grocery store so we decided to make a supper with bread, cheese, and apples and return to Bryant Park.

The temperature was in the eighties, much too muggy to search for a place to stay so we slouched overnight on the wooden benches in Grand Central Station. Later that night we heard the sounds of resident animals, rats and mice, the heavy breath of the Depression, and late night travelers. Blue Raven twice explained to police officers that we were combat veterans of the Bonus Expeditionary Force.

Star Boy was our platoon leader that early morning to face the first glance of sunlight, to ease the enemy way of the Depression, and when we returned to the main concourse there were five spectacular streams of sunlight through the high curved windows. Plucky danced from one great stream of natural light to the other, a great show of bright faces in a cavern decorated with elaborate stone curves, sculpted oak leaves, and shadows of acorns out of reach.

Star Boy stayed in the streams of sunlight, then turned slowly and counted the constellations painted on the curved ceiling. "The stars are reversed," he shouted and pointed to the scene of Biboon Ogichidaa, the winter warrior in a native totemic constellation that was otherwise named Orion the Hunter. "The warrior and three bright stars were painted in the position of Cancer." We turned slowly under the ceiling, counted out the constellations, and could not correct the star trace turnaround. The artist was obviously mistaken about the scene, or he painted the godly zodiac of winter in the summer. Blue Raven turned in circles and together we shouted out our praise of the artist for the tricky zodiac dream song, a concourse winter in the summer.

I was the platoon leader that morning in search of a campsite. We set out for Washington Square Park to find other bonus veterans, and we were told that natives had once camped near New York University. Park Avenue was an easy walk to Union Square, but we turned by mistake with the stream of people down Fourth Avenue toward Cooper Union. We should have walked down Broadway.

Fourth Avenue turned out to be a more relevant turn than the rumors of overnight natives because we walked directly into a corner store of chance stories. The Biblo and Tannen Booksellers, located on the corner of Ninth Street, became our source of information about native authors, art galleries, and overnight campsites in the city. Magazines and books were for sale on counters outside for ten cents. Plucky searched for military and adventure stories, and found a ratty copy of *Tarzan and the Apes* by Edgar Rice Burroughs. For several years since the series started he had turned the pages of discarded newspapers to read the comic strips of Tarzan.

I searched the shelves and random stacks inside the store for books by natives and any familiar authors, Herman Melville, Jack London, John Dos Passos, Sinclair Lewis, and found a copy of *Moby-Dick* and, of course, several copies of *Three Soldiers*. The books were stacked in the narrow aisles, and the scent of sweet tobacco and traces of mold wafted in the store, the pleasant signatures of a used bookstore.

Jack Biblo, one of the owners, surprised me with the declaration that, two years earlier, the novelist Sinclair Lewis had been awarded the Nobel Prize for Literature. Obviously he noticed the copy of *Main Street* in my hand, along with an early edition of *Moby-Dick*. I avoided the duty prize talk, and instead mocked the author because he had dismissed natives on the very first pages. Chippewas, Lewis wrote, once camped nearby, but they vanished with the flourmills and skyscrapers of Minneapolis. Carol Kennicott is the only one who vanished in the wearisome future of Gopher Prairie, not the Chippewas. There was no reason to open any novel with a dopey and romantic denigration of Chippewas.

The Nobel prizer probably did not know that native families were actually removed by the federal government to reservations. Chippewas were once translated and named in short histories, and ready to vanish in the second edition. "My native stories and dream songs are Anishinaabe, not Chippewa. So, you see we never vanished for any reason, and certainly never to please a leisure cruise novelist, rightly prized or not." I waved my arms and declared, "Listen, four native veterans of the war just invaded your bookstore."

"Where?" shouted Jack Biblo.

Plucky was outside and waved to the owner with a copy of *Tarzan and the Apes*. Star Boy, who was in the back of the store, shouted out his presence, came forward and saluted twice. He carried an original copy of *The Life, History, and Travels of Kah-ge-gah-bowh* by George Copway, one of the first Anishinaabe authors published by Weed and Parsons in 1847. Aloysius walked into the scene and greeted the owner with a notice of an art show at An American Place, a gallery located at 509 Madison Avenue.

"Nothing much surprises me in the book business, but the four of you in one morning, now that is not believable," he exclaimed. Biblo smiled, reached out to shake hands, and then teased, "So, are you buying books, camping in our store, or taking back Manhattan?" The tease was a perfect native moment, and naturally we returned the gesture with more teases.

"Yes, we want the store," said Star Boy.

"But, wait," declared Plucky, "you pay the rent every month and for that you can stay in the back and give me everything you have on Tarzan"

"We already live in the back," said Biblo.

"Why, trouble with immigration?" teased Plucky.

"Indians don't buy books, so we live here."

"Tarzan then, that's fair."

"One dollar for *Tarzan and the Apes*," declared Biblo.

"The sign said ten cents."

"The price has changed," teased Biblo.

"You can have the store back," said Plucky.

"Right, then the apes are free."

"So, what do we name our city?" asked Star Boy.

"Gopher Prairie," said Biblo.

"White Earth on the Hudson," said Blue Raven.

A few minutes later Biblo's partner came out of the back room with a cup of coffee. "Jack Tannen," he said, and that started a cascade of teases about the two Jacks. One Jack is never enough to run a bookstore.

"We both live in the back room," said Jack Tannen. "So, who wants a cup of coffee?" Four hands were raised, and we were directed to the back room secrets. There were two wooden chairs, one stool, and three unused cups, so my brother shared his coffee. The Jacks in turn asked us about the Depression on the reservation, the heartless vote of the Senate against the cash bonus for war veterans, and we told them about modern art and our move to Paris.

"Why Paris?" asked Biblo.

"Art, and memories of the war," said Blue Raven.

"New York is loaded with stories about the war, too much war chatter, and there are great modern artists, not Picasso or Matisse, but great painters, Arthur Dove, John Marin, and Georgia O'Keeffe," said Jack Tannen.

Jack Biblo mentioned that An American Place was a gallery owned by Alfred Stieglitz, the photographer and advocate of art, and his exhibitions included great modern paintings by Dove and O'Keeffe. "Listen to me, you should visit the gallery, and see for yourself the new abstract art, and more, Stieglitz is a brilliant photographer."

I told several stories about our service in the infantry, the death in combat of our cousin Ignatius Vizenor, and the great painters we met, Marc Chagall, Chaïm Soutine, Marie Vassilieff, and Moïse Kisling. The Jacks held back a natural tease of my casual boasts, so it was easy to continue with more about breakthrough authors, the great and subversive James Joyce, Guillaume Apollinaire, André Gide, Samuel Beckett, and Ezra Pound. Hard to believe that we met so many original artists and authors at Shakespeare and Company, the famous bookstore owned by Sylvia Beach in Paris. My brother became a distinctive artist there and his abstract blue ravens were exhibited in the Galerie Crémieux in Paris, and the same gallery published *Le Retour à la France: Histoires de Guerre*, my first collection of war stories.

"You didn't mention Marcel Proust," said Tannen.

"We never met him," said Blue Raven.

"Good thing, because he's dead, but not forgotten," said Tannen. "You should read *Swann's Way*, the first part of his huge *Remembrance of Things Past*."

"Why, what's the story?" said Blue Raven.

I was silent and not obliged to reveal my ignorance of Marcel Proust. Tannen handed me a copy of *Swann's Way* and told me the translation was very good, but to ignore the subtitle because some readers were not pleased with the weight only on the past. I searched the first chapter of the novel, a translation by C. K. Scott Moncrieff, for one or more memorable quotations.

"Great Paris gossip, gossip theory, really, the rich and creamy stories on the way to the First World War, and not a word about the noble Chippewas," said Tannen.

Biblo gestured for more stories, but then he turned away when a customer entered the store. He watched the customer for a minute, and then demanded more gossip theory about Paris.

"Do you want me to watch the desk?" asked Plucky.

"No need, there are more book lookers than book buyers, and there is a certain gesture and casual manner that reveals the browsers."

I read out loud a paragraph from *Swann's Way* about the circle of time, the remembrance of time. "When a man is asleep, he has in a circle round him the chain of the hours, the sequences of the years, the order of the heavenly host."

"Should have written about natives," said Plucky.

Tannen was so touched by my selection of the novel and the literary trace of connections in his own experiences, the hours and years in the bookstore, that he gave me the copy of *Swann's Way*.

We talked more about the gossip theory of Proust, and his association with so many notable writers and painters, but Biblo turned the conversation back to the modern art in New York City.

Arthur Dove was one of the great modern painters in the world, we were told that morning in the back room. "Go see his abstracts, the shapes and nature of colors, and you'll want to become a painter," said Jack Biblo.

Blue Raven did not directly respond to the painterly tease, but instead reached into his shoulder pouch and pulled out the Niinag Trickster to meet the two book Jacks.

"I am the brother of an artist, an erect abstract painter," said the hand puppet. The puppet head jerked from side to side, and then he stared, one by one, at the two booksellers. Biblo raised both hands and surrendered to the stares and teases. At that moment, the trickster puppet wagged his wooden penis three times. Everyone laughed, but the big laugh, the roar, was by Jack Biblo. "Manhattan is yours, take over the store, and give me a one way ticket to a reservation with puppets."

Biblo waited on a customer, but she wanted to sell not buy books. He lowered his head in silence, and bought two recently published books, *The Great Wall of China* by Franz Kafka and *The Good Earth* by Pearl S. Buck, for twenty cents. We frowned, and he exclaimed, "What, great books are turned over every day in the Great Depression."

Biblo was distracted with the woman who sold the new books because, he explained, she comes in every other week with two or more books. She either buys new books to read or she steals them from other bookstores. "She wears very smart clothes, hard to know by clothes because sometimes even poor people dress for better weather."

Biblo handed me a copy of *Look Homeward, Angel* by Thomas Wolfe, a new book he bought from the same woman a few weeks earlier, and told me that Sinclair Lewis praised the novel. "Read this novel, much more weighty and better written than *Main Street*, especially if you like big rumors and the regrets of a southern family."

I read out loud the first sentence from the epigraph of *Look Homeward, Angel*, "a stone, a leaf, an unfound door; of a stone, a leaf, a door. And all the forgotten faces," and continued with the end of the first sentence of the novel, "over the proud coral cry of the cock, and the soft stone smile of an angel, is touched by that dark miracle of chance which makes new magic in a dusty world."

"My brother must have that novel," said Aloysius.

"No, not for fifty cents?"

"Five times that new," said Biblo.

"Six hundred pages."

"Thirty cents," he muttered, "and no returns."

I continued to search the shelves and stacks for other titles, and decided to buy *All Quiet on the Western Front* by Erich Maria Remarque, published three years earlier, about the same time as *Look Homeward, Angel*. Biblo then handed me a copy of *Light in August* by William Faulkner. "Look at this novel, tricky talk about race, segregation, and ancestry, and some sort of curious class of outsiders in Mississippi." The novel had just been published, and probably was much too expensive, but he would negotiate the price.

I was enchanted with the straight scenes on the first page of *Light in August*. Lena went to town "six or eight times a year" by wagon and wore her shoes, but "would not tell her father why she wanted to walk in instead of riding. He thought that it was because of the smooth streets, the sidewalks. But it was because she believed that the people who saw her and whom she passed on foot would believe that she lived in the town too." That concise description alone was a trace of natural motion and tribute to liberty, and the very sentiments of natives in our family on the White Earth Reservation.

I tried to disguise my enthusiasm for the novel, set the two books aside, and changed the subject to the woman who read or stole books. Biblo, however, was a wise interpreter of gestures. He smiled and said, "I watched you read, drop the dopey pose, you like Faulkner."

"That was my best pose, so how much?"

"Fifty cents, these are new books," said Biblo.

"Manhattan and two new books for fifty cents, one about war and the other about liberty, now that is a very good deal in the Great Depression."

My brother told several stories about Dummy Trout and the gift of two puppets, but we decided earlier not to show the Ice Woman to anyone until we arrived in Paris. Tannen was curious about puppets and turned the trickster over and closely examined the fedora, carved head, leather chaps, breechclout, and wooden penis. My brother never allowed anyone to enter a hand or manipulate the head or penis of the Niinag Trickster.

Tannen apologized and explained, "I understand the character of puppet diplomacy." He paused, turned away, and then continued with stories about the puppet shows at the Modicut Puppet Theatre. Both Jacks were members of the Modjacot Shpeel Club, located near Union Square, only three blocks from the bookstore.

"Yiddish puppet theatre is very popular, and no one expected that reli-

gious and cultural satire of string puppets would find an audience," said
Tannen. Zuni Maud and Yosl Cutler, he recounted, created the puppet
theatre, but the owner of the building wanted to evict them because of
legal permits for huge audiences. The puppets actually testified in court
and the judge was so amused that he suggested the theatre become a club
to avoid the legal restrictions on public theaters.

Jack Tannen raved about the Modicut Puppet Theatre, but he never
considered natives with a tradition of puppets. Plucky mentioned the tin
heads and tattered puppets that Blue Raven created during the march of
the Bonus Army. "My favorite puppet was Herbert Tombstone, a rusty
condensed milk can head and twine fingers, who talked nonsense about
money, manners, and Andrew Mellon."

"Where is the president now?" asked Biblo.

"Aloysius left him with two other puppets on seats in the House of
Representatives," said Plucky. "Believe me, that was a very sad day, and
naturally the three puppets had to stay behind, Herbert Tombstone, Pozark Commie, and Wizard Oil, because that was the day the bonus ended
with the sudden death of a great veteran, Congressman Edward Eslick."

Biblo was excited and waved his hands, praised the creation of the
tin head president, and with great gestures described Herbert Hoover
in the Modicut Puppet Theatre. "Zuni and Yosl created five incredible
string puppets with grotesque features in a great satire of Mohandas Gan-
dhi, the salty nationalist, Ramsay MacDonald, the British prime minister, Léon Blum, the French prime minister, Vol Strit, the puppet of Wall
Street, and masterfully, the pudgy face of President Herbert Hoover."

Modicut was on tour in Russia and returned only a few weeks earlier,
but there were no productions scheduled at the theatre. Yiddish or not we
would attend any show of puppets in the city, and a few weeks later we
visited the theater and my brother was inspired with features of the string
puppets, the carved and plaster cast figures with moveable eyebrows and
mouths. The hand puppets were not the same, and the gestures were created with a finger rather than a string, but audiences easily grasped the
show of puppet stares and jerky moves.

Marc Chagall came to mind when we paged through a book of characters and puppets afloat on the page. Natives painted buoyant figures in

bright colors a century earlier, in ledger books, and the ancient rock and cave art depicted magical scenes in motion, waves of natural motion.

Jack Biblo told my brother to stand and show the Niinag Trickster to the hungry in the daily breadlines around the city, to "make some new satire with tin head puppets and mock the politicians, and do something to amuse the poor who shuffle away half the day in a dreary line for a fast meal, soup, potatoes, and bread."

Biblo was tired of the teases and directed us to depart for several breadlines, especially the McAuley Water Street Mission near the Brooklyn Bridge. Star Boy marched the platoon down Bowery through Chinatown to Pearl Street and Water Street. The breadline started in the gut and the hunger continued for several blocks. The McAuley Mission was easy to locate. The mission scene was downhearted, not a trace of familiar human motion on the slow and steady shamble to a daily meal. The tease and humor of a trickster puppet, or even a tin head commie or president, was not a conceivable scene that late muggy afternoon.

Jerry McAuley founded the New York Rescue Mission or the Helping Hand for Men in 1872. The mission provided a sense of solace for thousands of weary and lost souls, mean men on the run, and outcasts in search of trust and loyalty. Jerry, who earned the nickname, "Apostle of the Lost," was born in Ireland, became a street criminal in America, and was transformed by Christianity in Sing Sing Prison. His conversion was so admirable that the governor pardoned the newcomer of faith to serve others, and so the vision of his mission has been counted out every day by the hundreds of people who have the courage to stand in line for a meal. No godly demands, liturgy, or duties to creation were necessary to receive the care of the mission. The mission was honored in the sermons of Norman Vincent Peale. McAuley died in 1884, and the grace of chance and station has been carried out in the name of the Apostle of the Lost.

McAuley Mission was the formal name on the large extended business sign at 316 Mission Street. The policeman at the door ordered us to the end of the line, but we told him we were there as volunteers. My sense of ordinary humor was overwhelmed by the silent desperation, and there was an absolute absence of a native tease, literary irony, or satire. The mission was one of the last docks of mercy.

Eugene O'Neill enacted characters of torment, and he might have created the poetic wounds and heavy realism of hunger, and the rush of
silence in the first and last mission meals of the day. The want of others
at the front of the line caught in my throat, and my words were choked
when we met the superintendent of the mission. "Charity beats in every
good heart," he assured me, "but there were no duties at the mission that
would advance your position in the wait for dinner."

Fallacies overturn the charity.

Dummy Trout was mute by reason and lived with the native tease
of puppets, diva mongrels, and the voices of great sopranos. She came
to mind and slowly walked with me that afternoon back along the meal
line. I tried to catch the eyes of every person for two blocks, but hunger
dares not take the chance of care, a slight touch, or the unnatural tease
of sympathy. The street glance of a strange eye might weaken the spirit
of anonymity.

LIBERTY TRACE

The mayor of Hard Luck Town was seated on a box near a fire hydrant, and slowly shaving his face. Blue Raven and Star Boy saluted the bare chested mayor and that was the start of our new residence named the Liberty Trace near the East River in New York City.

Bill Smith was a sailor at heart, and with no ship or money at hand he had built the first shanty at the cobbled close of Tenth Street. The here and now town was near the river and the deserted shipyards, once a place of adventure and destiny on old Dry Dock Street.

Nellie the shanty mongrel panted at the side of the mayor. "She came from a respectable home somewhere to the cleanest jungle in the city," he said and then patted her on the head. "Nell came down here to live, and won't be shooed away."

Five neighborhood boys gathered around the fire hydrant, splashed in the water, and listened closely to the mayor take the measure of four native strangers. The boys studied our shoes, the blue ribbons on our shirt panels, and pointed at the ledger art book my brother carried.

Mayor Smith wiped his face, smiled, and then started that morning with his stories as a sailor, three times around the world, and ended with down and out anecdotes about the old shipyards on the East River. The great circle of his knowledge was learned at sea, and lasted with stories on land, a steadfast mayor of lonesome veterans camped on the cobblestones. Suddenly he was silent and stared at me first, then at my brother and cousins over the fire hydrant.

"I once sailed with Indians from Puget Sound," he said, and then turned toward the river. "They were brothers with high wave stories about ravens and bear walkers, and one story was about an Indian sailor who washed ashore in the last century and ended up as teacher of English in Japan."

"Queequeg on the whaler *Pequod*," teased Plucky.

"No, no, that was in the novel *Moby-Dick*."

"Professor Ranald MacDonald," said Blue Raven.

"Just, a weigh anchor story," said the mayor.

"MacDonald was related to the Chinook," my brother continued, "a native seaman and teacher with fur trade airs and graces that must have been a surprise to Commodore Matthew Perry."

"Where are you boys from?" asked the mayor.

"White Earth Reservation," said Plucky.

"Snowy country?"

"Northern Minnesota."

"Well, make this your new reservation in the city," he said and then pointed out a few other shanties at the end of the cobblestone close.

"This ain't no reservation," said Plucky.

"This is not paradise either, so build a slant shack or a house, plenty of loose metal and wood at the old docks and along the river, but remember we allow no commie talk, and we keep the place clean."

"Yes, sir," said Plucky.

"This is a trace of liberty," said Star Boy.

The Stars and Stripes waved on a pole in front of his shanty, and the mayor explained that every resident salutes the flag at reveille and retreat, and the flag is folded away at night. "This is a camp of patriots."

"Yes, sir," said Star Boy.

"We share the rations," said the mayor.

"Yes, sir," said Blue Raven.

Hard Luck Town was also named Hard Luck on the River, and the residents were only men, mostly Irish and Polish war veterans we learned later, although that would never explain the easy order and camaraderie. Only the two hard luck street names divided the rough and ready veterans, Jimmy Walker Avenue and Roosevelt Lane.

Liberty Trace was constructed and christened late that afternoon with heavy boards hauled out of the murky river, discarded blocks, packing crates, warped plywood, some dunnage afloat, and corrugated sheet metal that we swiped from the abandoned shipyard nearby. The mayor loaned me a hand saw to cut the heavy planks, and at the same time my brother cut several thick blocks of wood into the size of puppet heads. The shanty was secure enough from the rain, but our beds, two thick planks slanted over the worn cobblestones, were only slightly more comfortable than a park bench.

The mayor decreed we were shanty citizens.

My brother painted abstract blue ravens on totem boards mounted on each side of the entrance. That hurried and crude shanty became our solace and sense of liberty in the city. The other veterans had built more modern shanties, much more secure, and some with cooking stoves. The veterans constructed military style toilets, enclosures around a sewer, and narrow trenches near a warehouse. Pissing in the street, however urgent, was not allowed, and not only because the many nearby families were curious about the shanties of single men in Hard Luck Town. Luckily there was a floating bathhouse for the nearby community on the East River.

Bill Smith had been the first to build a shanty only a few weeks earlier, and he became the obvious mayor of the new town. He introduced the idea of communal meals, and shanty citizens who found a few hours of work shared the money for food. The second night we contributed heavy beef bones and dried beans for a stew, day old bread, and cheese to the communal town dinner. There were about thirty veterans there at the time, and every day two or three more shanties were constructed.

Monday, July 4, 1932, the Hard Luck Town veterans saluted at reveille the Stars and Stripes. Independence Day was celebrated with the thunder of cannons, one shot for each state of the Union, and repeated at six military posts in the metropolitan area. We heard the distant cannon booms at Governors Island, but not the ceremonial cannons at posts in the Bronx, Queens, or Staten Island.

The thick planks inside Liberty Trace were twisted and uncomfortable, and we hardly slept more than an hour at a time. So we were on the road very early that morning in search of natives, and makeshift mattresses. We walked south of Houston Street. The city was almost hushed. We heard only the steady clatter of milk wagons, and the slow paces of early smokers. An old man perched on a fire escape coughed, and two boys waved as we walked down the narrow streets, past the laundries, tailor shops, and closed stores. Later, we meandered on Delancey Street back to Bowery and then down Bleecker Street.

Plucky was the platoon leader that morning, and we followed an ingenious street cleaner with a water tank and rotary squeegee drawn by two horses. The country scent of wet horse manure lingered on the streets. Plucky turned at Mercer Street and then at Waverly Place to the entrance of Washington Square Park in Greenwich Village. Two older men were playing chess at that early hour, and the pesky pigeons waddled under the benches and pecked, and pecked, and pecked at nothing more than empty shadows. Weary and bearded men, some with hollow eyes, were stretched out on every bench in the park, and more were stranded in the wilted shrubbery waiting no doubt for the first glance of sunlight to ease the enemy way out of mind on that cloudy morning.

There were no traces of natives, not even a stray story about natives in the park or at New York University. The Bonus Army natives at the National Mall told me several times that night to ask about old Gray Face, a war veteran and regular native at Washington Square Park. No one had ever heard of Gray Face, or any natives, but at last one of the wise chess players pointed toward the two marble statues of George Washington on each side of the Memorial Arch. Yes, of course, we reached out to the stony gray president and then broke into wild laughter. Rightly we had been duped to carry out a trickster tease, and with the dopey trust that we might find natives in New York City.

Mayor Smith told me about the old street markets on Bleecker Street near Our Lady of Pompeii. The early church services on Independence Day had ended and parishioners were crowded around the vegetable carts. Star Boy bought carrots, cabbages, potatoes, onions, and rutabagas for a stew that night at the Hard Luck Town.

Blue Raven marched the platoon to more markets on Orchard and Essex Streets near Delancey Square. The Lower East Side was a constant rush of merchants, overcrowded tenements, and that grave sense of fault and frailty lingered in dark doorways, on rusty fire escapes, and on the grimy windows and pushcarts. Faces were badly worn, and the waves of misery reminded me of the war. So many bodies were wasted, hearts wounded by desertion, lungs weakened by poverty and disease. Young men wheezed, and old men panted on the streets.

Naturally we worried about health and the curse of tuberculosis. The white plague was a common disease on reservations. The Lower East Side was one of the poorest reservations in the world, and we could never again escape the obvious observation, that we were the fortunate natives compared to most of the poor people on the streets.

Plucky had found a comfortable pair of shoes in The Hut at Anacostia Flats, and searched for durable trousers, but could not find the right size. He would not be seen with rolled, rough cut, or frayed pants. We passed several carts of pants and at last entered S. Beckenstein's, World's Largest Pants Matching House, on the corner of Delancey and Orchard. London Shoes was next door, and across the street Grosoff Bros Haberdashers. Less than an hour later we each had a new pair of fitted and cuffed beige cotton gabardine trousers. We had never owned tailored pants, not even in the infantry. The pleated sturdy style would be our smart uniforms on the streets of New York City and Paris.

The only bright colors on the street were fruits and vegetables on the carts, hardly ever the lovely hues of blue or red billows in motion, nothing truly bright. The colors must have been reserved in the shadowy rooms on the other side of the tuberculosis windows. The men dressed in black and white, and with black hats or gray fedoras. The women wore cloudy aprons and peasant dresses. Most of the boys romped barefoot in the streets.

Jewish peddlers sold food and sundries on pushcarts parked in double rows on Orchard and Essex Streets in front of storefront merchants. Signs for Osterover's Smoked Fish, corsets, clothes, underwear, and eyeglass stores, with several signs printed in Hebrew. The vegetables were stacked on counters and carts. Women carried baskets and tin pails, and the negotiations were speedy and noisy.

Margaret, our mother, came to mind that morning at the street markets. She was a native herbal healer and used plants of various colors to cure, and to dye rose, mauve, and blue ribbons that she sewed to panels on our shirts. She was convinced that the display of color was protective and restored health, and she never hesitated to show her sons with at least a crease of natural color. We continued to wear the blue shirts our mother decorated with ribbons of color.

"The natural world of totems was never black," she declared when we were students at the government school, "sometimes cloudy, never black," but rather vibrant with the curative colors and hues of wild disguises. Yes, she used the same words to honor the actual natural disguises of birds, animals, and insects with poses of color and tricky masks. We rarely shared the notions of the protection, deception, and disguises of color with strangers. Margaret ordered us to wear blue ribbons on our infantry uniforms in the war, and would surely have rushed to brighten with color and ribbons the black and cloudy poses of people on the Lower East Side.

Plucky led our mattress mission on several market streets and we found eight thin and tattered square cushions apparently stuffed with horsehair. Two cushions on each of our bed planks, one for shoulders and the other for thighs, would make it possible to sleep most of the night. I started the negotiations with the pushcart owner, and declared that the price was even too much for new cushions, not the ragged, infested sacks for sale. The merchant was eager to part with the cushions, it seemed to me, and then in about fifteen minutes of avoidance the price was set at forty cents, or five cents for each cushion. We washed the cushions under the fire hydrant and beat them almost dry. No one complained that night about the moist scent of horsehair in the cushions.

Firecrackers were not permitted that Independence Day, and the police enforced the new declaration of quietus, a word we learned at the federal school on the reservation. The city was quieter with the Depression decree, and there were no accidents, fires, or deaths according to the hearsay over dinner in Hard Luck Town. The only noisy substitutes of celebration that day were the red snap crackers from Chinatown.

The rain glistened on the cobblestones, and some city events that afternoon were cancelled, but thousands of citizens gathered with their children at city parks for games and races in spite of the rain showers. Obviously we were envious of the potato races in the nearby squares because we would have run away with the vegetables for a communal shanty stew.

Star Boy was the platoon leader a few days later to the Alfred Stieglitz art and photography gallery, two blocks east of the Museum of Modern Art. Since the war my brother has avoided tunnels and ducked out of burrows and trenches, and his fear of narrow enclosures included the subway system, so we traveled that morning on the Third Avenue Elevated from Ninth Street to the gallery plainly named An American Place at 509 Madison Avenue.

Stieglitz was seated near a window at the side of the gallery, a portrait of a maestro of art with white hair and noble moustache, and with stacks of letters and a bloom of flowers on the desk. My brother paused only to admire a watercolor painting mounted nearby, *Downtown New York* by John Marin. The bloody sun, encircled with hues of blue and pale yellow, was a natural show between the abstract window frames and tracery of city columns and margins downtown.

The eminent photographer and impresario of modern art was either reserved or elusive when we entered, only a classy glance, and then he bowed his head without a word or slight gesture of directions. We slowly wandered around the gallery in silence, worried that even our hushed voices would be a distraction.

An American Place was a cozy sanctuary of art. The walls and ceiling were painted pure white, and the bright colors of the original paintings were heightened in the two chalky rooms, almost buoyant in the gallery. The larger room was painted completely gray, a shroud of overnight gray, cloudy ocean gray, memorable gray.

Blue Raven was enchanted with the sun bleached colors, the turn of wild blues, leathery greens, and abstract contours and natural shapes of the clouds and water by Arthur Dove. The modern spectacles of curves and color were named "a new realism" in the art talk of the city, the abstract scenes of nature, sun, clouds, and water. Dove had created abstract patterns and natural ornaments of motion and color.

My brother painted great irreducible blue ravens when he was a schoolboy, and the scenes were visual and totemic, not reductions or duplicates. Later he created more abstract and chancy blue ravens, scenes that deserted the customary contours of native totems, and showed the chancy traces of blue wings on a visionary landscape, the bright and broken claws over a city, or the heavy waves of blue ravens on the river Seine.

Blue Raven whispered as we turned a corner in the museum that new realism was inspired by the ancient pace of native art, on stone, bark, and paper, and the natural motion of cave art, "not the tidy search for cultural identity, no, new realism was a return to totemic visions of nature, the curves and color of the natural world." Then my brother traced silently with his fingers the magical silhouettes, the show of color and giant flowers, and the waves of heavy blues and dusty rouge mesas by Georgia O'Keeffe.

"Totemic fauvism and new realism were never the outcome of the war or stony reason, not creased or cubist abstract art," my brother continued to whisper as we moved once more through the chalky gallery. "The art of natural curves and colors is more than mere empathy, more than an apology for the ruins of nature, the rush of new realism has always been in the color, character, and totemic memory."

Plucky was on the other side of art, as he collected the words that show the deceit of abstract art, and the tease and tow of names in art history. "Blue Raven is a master of blue ravens," he boasted, and then teased the abstract scenes and colors with words. Plucky became a word painter when he named the hues of blues, and he invented new color names on the road, porter white, wizard blue, hunger brown, wheel rim blues, rusty blues, apron gray, cobblestone hues of gray, elevated gray, dog days rouge, and the natural sounds of blue memory. These new colors were in our memory, and his stories connected directly to the actual moments, and the abstract scenes were stories, "the words not the eye create the visual memory." Plucky roamed through galleries and whispered the words that created the art in his memory.

"Dove should paint blue ravens," said Star Boy.

"Chagall paints characters in blue flight, a rabbi under the wings of blue ravens," said my brother. "Blue waves and ravens are visionary, the words describe the scenes but not the visions."

Star Boy paused at the entrance and returned the classy glance with irony. Then one by one we nodded on our way out the door of An American Place. Plucky turned back and saluted but the gesture was not seen, and the exclusive gallery returned to the silence of Stieglitz. "Blue Raven might have painted ocean scenes, the abstract shiver and cut of nature in the city, and painted a raven wing bone at the very heart of a wild flower," said Star Boy.

The *Summer Exhibition* at the Museum of Modern Art presented selected works by French, American, and German painters, a survey of magnificent abstract art that included Paul Gauguin, Georges Braque, Henri Matisse, Vincent van Gogh, Moïse Kisling, Otto Dix, Paul Klee, and many other painters and sculptors.

Blue Raven was elated with the entire exhibition and noticeably moved in the actual presence of *The Praying Jew* by Marc Chagall, *Portrait of a Boy* by Chaïm Soutine, and *Head of a Woman* by Pablo Picasso. As an expressionist artist, my brother was always impressed with brush bruises, his description for thick layers of paint, and waves of color, blues and rouges, and he carried the rapture of the artistic scenes in visual memory.

Yes, we were courted by and obsessed with the waves of color, the sensuous pose, puckered lips, and facial blues of *Head of a Woman*. The slightest rouge on the right bare shoulder was an extraordinary presence that afternoon in the Museum of Modern Art. Pablo Picasso painted blue women for only a few years and long before the First World War. My brother was aware of the style and moody hues of blue hair and melancholy faces, but he concentrated on the nature and flight of blue ravens, and advanced the abstract totems and painterly tease of blues in the heart and character of natives.

Plucky declared that my brother never abandoned the blues and was never sidetracked by the sway of cubism or surrealism. "He pitched the honest blues, new, abstract and disguised in the nature of totems." Plucky carried on his care of my brother and the blues as we slowly moved to the portrait of an oval and enigmatic face with vacant eyes by Amedeo Modigliani.

"Aloysius Beaulieu and his modern blue ravens should be included in this exhibition," asserted Star Boy. Several nearby viewers smiled and turned away. We raised our hands in praise, of course, and then teased my brother about his fascination with rouge cheeks, painterly blue puckers, and sensuous waves of color.

Four natives circled *Girl with Blue Eyes* and in a cluster that excluded other viewers. We commented on the futile pale blue eyes, not an abstract scene or character portrait but a distortion of an apathetic woman with a high forehead, blank oval face, and the steady elongated necks of other portraits painted by Modigliani.

Blue Raven was the only artist to stay with the blues, and never painted lonely women. His comments were more about the curves and culture of color and brush of character than the plain counter creases of portraiture. "Modigliani painted the ordinary color of a blush on a slanted face with no cheek bones," said Blue Raven. "There, look at those bright red lips, probably a sexual pout, and the vacant eyes of torment, the haunted gaze of an absence."

"Yes, the gaze of the dead," said Plucky.

"No, the gaze of Modigliani," said Star Boy.

Blue Raven was fascinated with the clumsy and distorted characters painted by Chaïm Soutine. I told our cousins as we sauntered to the next room that Nathan Crémieux, the gallery owner in Paris, told us many stories about La Ruche in Montparnasse, the dirt cheap hive of wild and marvelous painters, sculptors, and poets, Marc Chagall, Moïse Kisling, Fernand Léger, Jacques Lipchitz, Blaise Cendrars, Guillaume Apollinaire, and others.

Later we viewed the Modigliani portrait of Soutine. The elongated features were slightly jowly, bloated nose, blushed, and with droopy eyes. Soutine, we were told, was distant and elusive. Luckily we attended an exhibition of his early paintings at the Galerie Bing in Paris about five years earlier, a few months before we returned to the reservation for the second time.

The Museum of Modern Art exhibition had opened a month earlier and was very popular. We moved slowly with the crowds to the display of *Portrait of a Boy,* with the skewed eyes, mighty ears out of balance, and great blunt hands, a perfect disharmony. Soutine painted ordinary characters with natural distortions that touched the very heart of creation and irony. The expressionistic boy was caught in the comedy of culture, and appeared rather cocky in a red vest. The brush traces and texture of paint created a sense of motion. Soutine painted a boy in blue, an altar boy, choirboy, room service boy, pageboy, boy with cap, and many boys in blue.

The great rave came much later with hand gestures, when my brother simulated the uneven touch of rouge on the face of the boy, and the heavy red vest painted by Soutine. The contrasts of blue in the background of the scene were either the shadows of stormy waves or blotchy hues of mountains and created a boy afloat in space.

"The background is planetary blue," said Plucky.

The Marc Chagall painting, *The Praying Jew*, sometimes named *The Rabbi*, was mounted in a position that seemed to dominate the entire space, and viewers were hushed by the image of Judaism. The painting was about three feet wide and four feet high. The Jew wore prayer clothes, shawl, and leather phylacteries, and was painted mostly in black and white, with only slight fleshy rouge on the angular face and hands. The lower lip was brighter, and the weary eyes were distant, an ancient gaze that reached past the viewers and outside the museum. Chagall, we learned later, had painted an old man, a beggar, dressed in the prayer clothes of his father. The artist had bright and spirited eyes, but the old beggar was a captive of destiny, and yet the artist created a gaze of visionary liberty.

Blue Raven told stories about our visit with Chagall and his wife Bella at a studio in Paris shortly after they had returned from Russia. Some of his paintings were stacked against the wall, and we saw the originals of *The Birthday, Blue Horses, I and the Village*, and many more.

"Chagall was invited to the exhibition of my abstract blue ravens and wounded veteran series, *Corbeaux Bleus, Les Mutilés de Guerre, Nouvelles Peintures par Aloysius Hudon Beaulieu*, at the Galerie Crémieux in Paris," my brother said as we started our return walk down Fifth Avenue. Plucky repeated the names several times to practice his French.

The temperature reached the nineties that week, and the floating bathhouse was crowded with children, so we built a rough and ready cover and watched the boats on the East River. Blue Raven outlined three new puppet heads, and that afternoon on the river he started to carve the first caricatures of Léon Blum and General Philippe Pétain, the Lion of Verdun. He carved with the same knife that he had used in combat. Odysseus, the great reservation trader, gave each of us a Hammer Brand Elephant Toe Pocket Knife when we enlisted as infantry soldiers fourteen years ago. My brother had carved so many wooden pendants the pick bone amber was worn smooth.

Plucky teased my brother, "General Pétain would not like his head hollowed out by a native veteran with nothing more than a pocketknife."

"Marshal Pétain the hand puppet," said Star Boy.

"The war is over," said Blue Raven.

"Pétain would agree that a hollow wooden head is much better than the fate of a rusty condensed milk can named Herbert Tombstone," said Plucky.

"Hoover is a waste of wood," said Blue Raven.

Star Boy promised the mayor of Hard Luck Town a copy of *Moby-Dick* by Herman Melville, so a few days later on a cool morning we returned to Biblo and Tannen Booksellers. "I knew you boys could not stay away," said Biblo. "Where did you land that first night, at Camp Thomas Paine?"

"No, too far away," said Plucky. "Mayor Smith invited us to build a shanty at Hard Luck Town on the East River. Patriotic place, reveille, retreat, camp meal plan, and mostly veterans who keep the place clean."

He touched our shoulders, one by one, and then waved us to the back room of the store where he handed me a copy of *Dawn Boy: Blackfoot and Navajo Songs* by Eda Lou Walton. I opened the small limited edition book with care and read out loud one of the songs, "The Lights."

> *the sun is a luminous shield*
> *borne up the blue path*
> *by a god*
> *the moon is the torch*
> *of an old man*
> *who stumbles over stars*

Biblo was enchanted with the beauty of the concise poetic images, and yet he wondered how the editor had favored the songs in poetic translation, and "who were the original singers, and how were the songs recorded and transcribed?" Serious questions, of course, that he did not hesitate to answer that afternoon, "Truly, what does it matter, the songs touch the heart from the desert to my bookstore, and who dares to write about the poetry by Indians?"

E. P. Dutton and Company published *Dawn Boy* six years earlier, and only seven hundred and fifty copies. Biblo said he bought the copy from an older man "who told me that Eda Lou Walton, the editor, teaches literature at New York University."

"We were there last week, at Washington Square Park looking for old Gray Face," said Plucky. "Maybe Eda Lou knows where to find the natives in New York."

"Gray Face, a relative?" asked Biblo.

I changed the subject and returned to the lovely book of native songs. Biblo told me the book was a rare edition and cost only a dollar. He pointed out the clean pages and tight binding, and he knew, of course, that the actual price once we teased and dickered would be mine, fifty cents.

Thomas Wolfe was on my mind that morning, but we could not get past the serious talk about native poetry. The metaphors were cultural and close to nature, and that raised the expectation that natives would have a better ear for and greater sensitivity to the images, and we were moved, of course, but Blackfoot and Navajo poetry in translation was not Ojibwe or Anishinaabe.

"Japanese songs are not French," said Blue Raven.

Plucky intruded on cue and declared that the author should publish a collection of Anishinaabe dream songs, "and here is the title, *The Sky Loves to Hear Me Sing*."

"Go ask her yourself," said Biblo. He seemed irritated and insisted that we should contact her directly. "Why not, and ask her to sign the book, no better reason than that to call on an author, and especially a professor."

Plucky was the natural platoon leader and we marched back to Washington Square Park in search of the romantic editor of the mesa dawn boys, and actually found her name listed in the directory of the College of Arts and Science.

The office door was open, and a breeze through the open window carried the scent of perfume into the hallway. Professor Walton was reading a manuscript at her desk, and did not notice four natives at the door. I tapped the glass with my finger, and without looking up she told me to enter. There, we observed her at work, and without the hesitation of eye contact. She was a small woman, and wore heavy gold jewelry on her neck and wrists. Maybe she painted too much rouge on her face that morning, and for a moment she became a portrait by Modigliani.

Professor Walton raised her head and with a strong voice said, "You are not my students, so why are you here without an appointment?"

I handed over *Dawn Boy* and asked her to autograph the book. "Jack Biblo the bookseller secured the book for me, and told us you were a professor."

She firmly told us to sit down, but there were only two chairs and a second desk. Plucky and Blue Raven sat on the wooden desk near the door, and then she surprised us with the question, "Where in the world are you going?"

"Paris, and the world of art," said Plucky.

"American Indians?"

"Yes, and we are war veterans from the White Earth Reservation and soldiers in the Expeditionary Bonus Force," said Star Boy. He was very formal, and in turn asked, "And where in the world are you going?"

Professor Walton burst into laughter, and her voice was loud for a small woman. Ordinary hand gestures rattled the jewelry on her wrists. She smiled and said she appreciated the retort. "You know, of course, that literature is a journey, and today this is my journey with an immigrant, a Jewish boy on the Lower East Side in *Call it Sleep*, an unpublished novel by Henry Roth."

"What native songs do you sing?" asked Plucky.

"None," she responded with no hesitation, and then explained that she was the editor of the collection not the actual author or translator of the native poems. "The poems are personal only because of my gratitude."

"Why not Anishinaabe poems," said Plucky.

"Frances Densmore translated and published those songs, as you probably know, and the book was published by the Bureau of American Ethnology," said Eda Lou.

"Yes, we met her, and some of our relatives were the singers she recorded, as you probably know," said Star Boy.

"Where are the natives?" asked Blue Raven.

"The Mohawks are out of work, and around here there are only the pretenders, but why would you ask me?"

I told her the story about the native tease and search for old Gray Face in Washington Square Park, "and at last only a gray chess player understood the tease and pointed at the statues of George Washington."

"What else are you reading?" she asked me.

"*Look Homeward, Angel* by Thomas Wolfe."

"Yes, nostalgia for home and angels." Eda Lou pointed at the second desk near the door and said, "There, you might want to know, that was his desk, and we shared the office for several years, but he left two years ago to write another novel."

"Why nostalgia?"

"Southern strain of class, brands, and breeds, and not the struggle of immigrants," declared the professor. "Not only southern angels, as you know, but the northern strain of manners and moods in *Main Street* and the shallow satire of bourgeois boredom in *Babbitt* by Sinclair Lewis."

"The Nobel Prize for manners and moods, the perfect notice of dopey class scenes," I said, but she was apparently distracted by our presence and the talk about nostalgia in popular novels.

"Read *Call it Sleep*," she whispered with emphasis and then raised the manuscript in one hand. "Leave the angel stories to the readers on cruise ships."

Eda Lou became our platoon leader and marched four natives to the entrance of the building. She touched my face and handed *Dawn Boy* back to me, and rightly without an autograph as the editor.

Eda Lou returned to *Call it Sleep* by Henry Roth.

A few days later we read an advertisement in the *New York Times* that transatlantic rates on the French Line were "the lowest since 1914." The fare was much less expensive than our first cruise ship passage to France. We could not decide on a date, only because we were at ease in our shanty the Liberty Trace, and with the memorable veterans in Hard Luck Town.

Friday, July 29, 1932, steady rain that morning and much heavier later in the day. The rainwater ran over the cobblestones and under our shanty. The Liberty Trace was home but public cover was more secure and necessary that day. Blue Raven was our platoon leader and we quick marched to the Third Avenue Elevated and doubled our pace to Fifth Avenue and the New York Public Library.

Star Boy headed directly to the newspaper room and a few minutes later he returned with the tragic news that two Washington policemen had shot and killed our good friend, William Hushka, and another bonus veteran, Eric Carlson, yesterday, Thursday, July 28, at a government building near the Federal Triangle. Hushka was shot in the heart, and he died in service to the Bonus Expeditionary Force.

Nothing personal about the bonus veterans would be remembered in a generation, nothing but the numbers of veterans in the Bonus March, the revised numbers of spectators, the tidy counts of politicians, presidents, and favors of insiders, and the generals who were always advanced in rank for chancy and deadly maneuvers, and the shooters who executed their duties, with a few names almost forgotten in memorial stories.

Naturally we worried about our friends, and that night over a dinner of potato, carrot, and beef bone soup with heavy dark bread, we shared the tragic stories with other veterans at Hard Luck Town. The veterans at the retreat saluted the memory of the bonus veterans who had been put to rout by young soldiers, and when the Stars and Stripes was folded we shouted out the names of William Hushka and Eric Carlson.

My head and shoulders were wet with rain, but we could not return to our shanty. We marched in silence for several hours that night and came to rest on the cold stone base of the statue of General Giuseppe Garibaldi, the warrior of independence, in Washington Square Park.

"Tonight is the end of our road as bonus veterans, and once more we need more than a sunrise to ease the enemy way," said Star Boy.

"Liberty Trace was an adventure," said Plucky.

"Hushka was our native brother," said Star Boy.

"A native outsider," said Blue Raven.

"Paris on the next boat," shouted Plucky. He turned and repeated the declaration in my direction, and waited for the good word of our departure. We marched back to our shanty and in the light of a candle checked the schedules of ship departures.

July 30, 1932, we saluted the Stars and Stripes at reveille and then announced to the veterans that we would depart that day for France. We conferred the ownership of our shanty, the Liberty Trace, lock, stock, and totems, to the mayor, and granted him the right to pass on the shanty to the next veteran who arrived at Hard Luck Town.

Plucky hailed a taxicab that morning to West Fifteenth Street and Pier 57 near the National Biscuit Company. Taxi fares were hardly more than the subway because of the Depression, and drivers were eager to find passengers. The *Ile de France* was scheduled to depart at noon. We arrived two hours early and the dock was already crowded with passengers.

Star Boy slowly counted out three hundred and seventy dollars, less than a hundred dollars each, for the one way passage of four natives on the *Ile de France*. The regular single rate for tourist class was two hundred dollars.

Night of Tributes

By Now traveled with a haversack, an army blanket, and a pup tent. She painted a blue raven on one side of the shelter to honor her cousin, and a red cross on the other side. She camped on the dusty back roads near forests, fields, and riverbanks, and bivouacked overnight on farm porches and barns close enough to hear the breath of her trusty mount Treaty.

The National Mall was crowded so she pitched the pup tent near the street and ruins of Federal Triangle. The grass was thicker there, under the shade trees, and a natural place to rein Treaty. The pup tent was a station in the night, a port with no promise, but not a residence, and in a heavy rain she moved to an abandoned building nearby. The veterans were always ready to tease with an overnight invitation on a canvas covered straw bed, and she was always ready with a speedy retort, "Treaty, my horse, would eat your straw bed before you could get out of your pants." The veterans teased her sometimes about sex only to hear the speedy original counters.

Army nurses learned how to divert fantasies.

The veterans gathered at breakfast and supper at more than thirty sites in the city, and the entire social muster was connected to meals, not tents. By Now was one of the few nurses in the Bonus Army, and she was the only veteran who lived in a pup tent. Most veterans pushed back the recollection of army pup tents and trenches, and built bold and stately tent mansions with large sections of canvas and other materials.

By Now, however, revised the pleasure of pup tents when she started to share the touch and tease of William Hushka, the migrant butcher and veteran from Chicago who was born in Lithuania. By Now and Hushka were always together at supper, and the gestures of stories were personal, and with a sense of irony the native nurse would tease the migrant every night on the brick bench at sunset. She mocked his accent, teased his gentle manner and tender touch as a butcher, and never mentioned the war. The constant murmur of their voices at every sunset was the show and motion of intimacy, and a pup tent was not the natural outcome.

Treaty neighed with the coos and murmurs.

Hushka never seemed to be in a hurry, and his stories were naturally slowed with the pleasures of memories, but the presence of a native nurse hurried his stories, hurried the vegetable talk at supper, and then slowed down on the brick bench for the sunset. He pretended to plead for the sunset to slow down, wait, wait another minute. That was the steady show for his native lover By Now Rose.

Treaty was content with the sweet grass under the shade trees on the boulevard, and every day she was mounted for familiar tours of the National Mall and the other campsites of the Bonus Army. Several times a week the children waited for the sound of the steady clop clop of heavy hooves on the wooden drawbridge to the Anacostia River.

Superintendent Glassford made similar rounds of the camps on his motorcycle, and Treaty turned her ears and recognized the sound of the engine at a distance. At every chance encounter, almost every day, the superintendent touched the wagon horse on the nose, and then ran his hand slowly down her neck.

"Treaty is a champion with the veterans," Glassford said many times, and then he told stories about the horses at West Point, the United States Military Academy. By Now in turn told stories about her service as a combat nurse, and her loyal mount named Black Jack.

Hushka had many friends at the other camps, and he meandered that morning to Anacostia Flats. By Now mounted Treaty and trotted over the wooden drawbridge to the river. Treaty high stepped in the shallows, and then plunged her head into the cool water. By Now invited two or three children on each visit to mount Treaty and circle a row of shanties and The Hut.

Hushka talked with Anthony Oliver about a boxing event to support the Bonus Army, and then feigned a few punches with his boys Nick and

Joe. Nearby, Alfred Steen was prepared to pose for a newspaper photographer in his sensational "burial case." By Now mentioned that she had seen him earlier in the makeshift mausoleum, "the boast of a tombstone veteran."

"Bonus Soldier" was printed at the bottom of the mock burial stage. Alfred wore a white shirt and tie, and he was stretched out on a raised platform over the notice, "The most of us will be dead by 1945." The sign was an obvious reference to the delayed bonus. Congress had approved a bonus, a Tombstone Bonus, he repeated over and over, that would be delayed by twenty years. "We want employment not charity," was another message printed on the simulated coffin. Alfred played out the tombstone scene with a great sense of humor.

Thursday, July 28, 1932, William Hushka, and another bonus veteran, Eric Carlson, were shot and killed near the Old Armory and the Federal Triangle. More than a hundred police were ordered to close that section in the morning, and later that afternoon the veterans moved to recover the area. Police were pelted with bricks, and two officers panicked in the mayhem and fired pistols at the veterans.

Hushka was shot in the heart and died alone in the ruins of bricks and dusty debris of the city. By Now had mounted Treaty in the morning and crossed the drawbridge to the river at Anacostia Flats. She mourned for months that she was not there to distract the police or to nurse her generous lover from Lithuania. She imagined his last tender glance, the bloody white shirt, and the last touch and slow whisper that summer afternoon.

Hushka must have been shot without cause, murdered by the police, because the veteran would never menace the police or anyone. William was always ready to march with dignity and shout out the matter and cause of veterans, and rightly protest for a cash bonus, but he would never threaten the police.

Hushka was an honorable veteran.

Superintendent Glassford waved to the veteran and migrant butcher almost every day as he toured the many camps on a motorcycle, and whenever he stopped near the Federal Triangle, they talked about the rage of Germany and the independence of Lithuania at the end of the First World War. Hushka was a migrant of destiny. He sold his butcher shop, gave the money to his wife, enlisted in the infantry, and served with one of the first units ordered into combat in France.

General Douglas MacArthur, the army chief of staff, and his aide in high tight boots, Major Dwight Eisenhower, commanded an armed military assault against the peaceful combat veterans. MacArthur ordered the soldiers to use tear gas and bayonets, chase the veterans out of the city, and then destroy with tanks and fire the huts, shacks, wickiups, and exotic shanties of the Bonus Expeditionary Force.

The Bonus March ended with the rout of veterans, but the shame of the president and soldiers would last forever. The veterans returned to homes, hovels, and abandoned boxcars, and lived with the truth stories of poverty and the camaraderie of veterans.

By Now and Treaty returned to the Federal Triangle that afternoon and on the way saw columns of armed soldiers near the Capitol Building. Later, tanks and soldiers with gas masks invaded the camps on the National Mall and burned every flagpole and trace of veterans down to ashes on the bare ground.

Later that night the army crossed the drawbridge and with bayonets the soldiers forced the veterans and their families to leave the camp and city. The soldiers set fire to Anacostia Flats, burned the Stars and Stripes as a political siege of vengeance, and destroyed the library at The Hut. That night the national capitol was a war zone, a siege of disgrace against the peace and humor of veterans, and the smoke lasted for several days. The stories of the military siege were told on the reservation, on dusty roads and in farm families, and around the world.

President Herbert Hoover dined alone that night, and must have witnessed the glow of fires on the National Mall and Anacostia Flats. General MacArthur invaded the camps of honorable and decorated war veterans only to protect the president from the inequities and desperate poverty of the Great Depression.

Tuesday, August 2, 1932, By Now was one of three veterans and the military honor guard present for the burial ceremony of Private William Hushka at Arlington National Cemetery. He was born in Lithuania in 1895, served in the Forty-First Infantry Division in France, and died as a veteran in the Bonus Army on July 28, 1932.

By Now touched each letter of his name engraved in the white stone, and then leaned close on the marker until sunset, a night of tributes. The director allowed her to stay overnight at the cemetery. At sunrise she mounted Treaty and returned on the same dusty roads back to the native tease and stories of Bad Boy Lake and the White Earth Reservation.

Ritzy Motion

The *Ile de France* was pushed away from Pier 57 with the hurrahs of ritzy motion on Saturday, July 30, 1932, and then the luxury ocean liner steamed slowly down the Hudson River past the Statue of Liberty and Governors Island.

Star Boy was our platoon leader for the departure, and we marched straightaway to the starboard deck and saluted twice the absence of a statue on Staten Island. A few smart tourists were curious about our tribute to the borough, and together we told stories about the ridiculous proposal of a giant statue of a native warrior with a war bonnet and peace pipe, and one bronze hand raised upright as a gesture of welcome to newcomers, migrants, tourists, and fugitives to the irony and liberty of the United States of America.

Some passengers remembered the news reports when President William Howard Taft, Rodman Wanamaker, and federal agents dedicated an enormous memorial monument and sculpture to the vanishing race. But the memorial had faded away by the start of the First World War. Star Boy pointed out the obvious irony that only the crazed notion of the bronze giant vanished without a trace.

The Indian Head nickel was struck by the United States Mint and issued for the first time to those who attended the groundbreaking political carnival of the National American Indian Memorial at Fort Wadsworth on February 22, 1913, including some thirty native leaders from reservations. The natives were advised to sign a treaty of civilization, but the great deal was nothing more than fealty and the concession of native territory and liberty.

The portly president and generous department store baron passed away, and not a trace of the memorial strategy remains, but the new nick-

els were in hand, easy change in any market, and the warrior natives never vanished.

We told the tourists on deck that afternoon that more than twenty
thousand natives had served in the First World War, mostly in the infantry, and their casualties were much higher than for other soldiers, and
we honored the name of our cousin who had died in combat near Mont-
bréhain and the Hindenburg Line.

Four natives in new gabardine trousers saluted the memory of Private
Ignatius Vizenor, and then, as the mighty *Ile de France* churned ahead
into the transatlantic waves, we explored the deck levels and salons and
decided that the lower covered deck at the stern was our station, out of
the flow of the tony tourists. The deck steward reserved four chairs and
then pointed to the open overhead deck. He jiggled his head and described the seaplane catapult, an incredible cruise ship mail service. The
plane was actually catapulted into the air over the ocean to deliver a few
tourist postcards on land. The catapult mail service reduced the delivery
time by one day, but was too expensive and lasted for only two years.

The art deco steamship was decorated with modern designs, easy
curves, and ornamentations. Plucky opened his arms to the nude statues
in the salon several times on our tours. There were two ordinary beds in
our cabins, but some of the ritzy cabins were enhanced with elaborate
contours, painted flowers, and graceful trees, and at every turn we might
have oohed and aahed over the classy patterns of balance and manners
on the ocean liner. Only the lifeboats were substantial and ordinary. The
three funnels were painted hard red with a black banner.

The tourist class cabins were once considered second class, and the
new class came with a reduction of fares to entice new passengers during the Depression. Truly, we were enticed by the price, and the service
and meals were extraordinary on the voyage. Naturally, we compared the
stately dinners in motion to the pot-au-feu of veterans on the cobblestones in Hard Luck Town.

The other services on the six-day journey included a huge chapel with
gothic style pillars, a shooting gallery, a gymnasium, and curved wooden
deck chairs. Yet, despite the favors and comforts we looked back a few
times and told stories to overcome the culture and demeanor of the

cruise, stories about our shanty of liberty, reveille, retreat, moody veterans and the camaraderie of the Bonus Expeditionary Force.

Ritzy motion was a natural native tease.

Our tourist cabin station restricted access to some decks and sections of the ship, of course, but we managed to tour by invitation and by stealth most of the premier outposts of social status. The Terrace Café was reminiscent of Le Dôme Café in Paris, a classy imitation, but not with the envy and steady tease of artists and poets on the run, and never with the constant stench of bodies, perfume, paint, cigarettes, and house wine.

Thomas Wolfe and *Look Homeward, Angel* were hardly the subjects of casual conversations in the salons or on deck, so my mockery of southern nostalgia was sidelined by the steady chitchat about cuisine and the wine terroir, political factions at the Democratic National Convention in Chicago, and the nomination of Governor Franklin Delano Roosevelt of New York for president of the United States.

Mostly the weather was clear the first few days, and in the afternoons nearly all of the passengers were reclined on deck chairs with only a few unread cruise books at hand. The most common were *The Good Earth* by Pearl Buck, and *Years of Grace* by Margaret Ayer Barnes.

Practically every woman on deck wore a cloche hat, and most of the men wore ivy or newsboy caps. Our gray fedoras were rolled and out of shape, and might have blown away on the windy decks, but we wore the creases with pleasure at the very poses of high cruise customs.

The wind and waves were deceptive and treacherous, and our best stories were moored, out of class, and yet every season, storm, disease, and war became our duty in native stories. We were at sea with a distant but lenient culture that would never survive the reservation or the lusty stories of winter with the Ice Woman.

I was out early every day, selected a deck chair at the stern of the ship, and created scenes for more stories about the Lower East Side, Jack Biblo, Eda Lou Walton, Thomas Wolfe, and, of course, the Bonus Army, William Hushka, and By Now at the Federal Triangle and Anacostia Flats. The ocean waves were wide and steady, hardly noticeable, and traces of the wake continued at a great distance behind the ship. The constant rush of the screw and vibration of the engines were more obvious at the stern. The sensation of the steady sounds set me afloat in dreams, not sleep, but that discrete sense of reverie, a natural source of native dream stories.

Natives were created in dreams and truth stories, the tease and chance of creation, and the natives we admired were never on the road in any season without a sense of chance and stories. Natives were hardly secure with mere names, not even the tease of worldly surnames of ancient fur traders, but dream names were always changeable in stories about creation, the winter, war, art, literature, and deadly poverty.

We pretended that most natives were dreamers and teachers, hunters and traders, creative painters and storiers, and better storiers because not many natives at the time were commercial farmers or shopkeepers, mechanics, railroad engineers, sailors, mercenaries, missionaries, butlers, professors, doctors, and yet natives outlasted the constant turns of economic depression, forecasts of poverty, and, of course, the corruption of federal policies. We created original and ironic dream stories of the Depression and the chance of native feats in the early cruise liner class of the enemy way.

The family newspaper, exotic traders, railroads and hotels, telephones and radios, art and literature, the last great war, diva mongrels and the tricky hand puppets were the sources of our circle of knowledge, the chance of spirited encounters, and once more the mighty ocean was another chance of native dream stories.

Blue Raven was a nickname, not a sacred or given dream name. Aloysius wondered if he might have been a dream or sacred name of a nun at the mission. "My name might have been one of the blanket dream names of priests and saints, Ignatius and Aloysius."

My brother dreamed of ravens as a child, told dream stories about ravens, and he imitated the chatter and shouts of ravens in the bare winter birch. He was inspired with the dream flight of a great blue raven over the mission and hospital, and the blue drifts of a winter storm were the shadows of blue ravens in his dream stories. There were no clouds, only the great shadows of blue raven wings over the White Earth Reservation.

Dream stories were original, of course, and no two natives ever told the same dream stories. Debwe truth stories were never mere recitations or repetitions. Even creation stories were related with a sense of chance, not memorized or constant and studied as liturgy. The truth stories were creative and ironic, as truth stories must be ironic because the last story has never been told, and always with the native tease of sincerity.

The ocean waves inspired dream stories.

Truth stories were necessary to stay afloat.

Clergy Dust, a small woman of the cloth, arrived one spring afternoon on a horse from the east some thirty years ago. She may have been born native, and the stories she told about dream treaties were quirky and conceivable as stories once told by shamans, but the treaties she dreamed and preached were terminal, end of the road stories, and the outcomes were scriptural salvation, not a native sense of chance in creation stories.

Not many natives on the reservation ever trusted the preacher or her treaty dreams. She was mocked, and that was our fun as boys, but even so we were wary and only once or twice dared to shout out the names Dirt Talker or Dream Cheater.

My mother was very direct about the dream cheaters and never hesitated to mock the preacher, "What was the tense of your dream treaty?" My favorite story was the night at the Leecy Hotel when my mother saw the dream cheater in the lobby and asked her, "Dream me the native pronouns of your peace treaty." The hotel visitors burst into laughter, but the constant teases never seemed to worry Clergy Dust.

The dreams we cared about were creative stories that were told and recreated with many versions. No one would listen to the last stories, because only the despots told final stories. The old condition of the words, verbs, and nouns of treaties and the many treaty promises and hesitations of federal agents were ironic, but never, never dream stories.

Shamans and the great native visionaries would, as a game, only reveal in stories the catch and release words of a new daydream, or delight and mock a treaty on a summer night. Likewise no sober citizen, lawyer, poet, or president would pretend to own the many dream stories and circles of knowledge that created the Declaration of Independence.

Clergy Dust was dedicated and at times admired with sympathy for her awkward resistance to the steady and cruel teases of natives. So many other dream cheaters had arrived in the worst of times and tested natives, our family and friends, and then moved on to a better scene of treaty conversions.

Dummy Trout created only one dream cheater hand puppet, but she could not mimic the gestures of fake treaty promises, or the terminal shows of priests and missionaries. Dream cheaters were persistent and foreseeable, and present in every word and sentence of the past and future, and that was the natural motion of native irony. The spirit of native doubt, contradiction, and irony has already overturned the dream treaties of the most obvious cheaters. Native trickster stories, however, revealed the dream cheaters with demon masks, hand puppets, and the tender hoax of faint praise. The White Earth Reservation sustains contradictions and traces of irony and truth stories.

About the Author

Gerald Vizenor is the author of more than twenty books
of nonfiction, fiction, and poetry. He attended college
on the G.I. Bill after serving in the armed forces for
three years, mostly in Japan, and studied at
New York University, Harvard University,
and the University of Minnesota.
He is Anishinaabe and a citizen
of the White Earth Nation
in Minnesota.